I0712414

Devils That Prey

Devils That Prey

A Novel

By

David Washburn

ISBN (Trade Paperback): 979-8-9866624-0-4
ISBN (eBook): 979-8-9866624-1-1
ISBN (Hardcover): 979-8-9866624-3-5

Devils That Prey

Cover Design by Getcovers.com
Edited by Kaylynn Wurzelbacher

This story is a work of fiction and inspired by an overactive imagination (and let's be honest, probably anxiety) while driving home from Myrtle Beach, where my family and I stopped to get gas and use the restroom at a very suspicious, outdated, and downright grimy gas station in South Carolina, miles from the highway. The little corners of America that time leaves behind are the inspiration for this novel.

Published by Burn Ward Publishing

Instagram: @WashburnWrites
TikTok: @WashburnWrites
Email: DavidWritesStories@gmail.com

Published in the United States of America.

1 2 3 **4** 5 6 7 8 9

1

◇

Everyone sits under the warm fluorescent lights as the buzzing from the burning-out bulbs hum a chorus along with the tension in the air. The people in the room sit in silence, darting their eyes to the salt-and-pepper-haired man sitting at the head of a wooden picnic table, eating, as they wait for him to *maybe* speak. There are at least two dozen people seated at several cafeteria style picnic tables, feasting on meat with their bare hands like chicken wings. No one is speaking, just the sound of chewing and the lights humming.

The tension is thick and some sit, picking at their food with looks of disappointment plastered onto their faces. Others sit there eating their food quickly, as if there may be a prize for the first to finish their food. The man at the head of the table sits stoically, anticipating someone to speak. He shoots glances around the room as if he is challenging someone, anyone, to address the elephant in the room.

One gentleman sitting at a table near him, wearing a red flannel button-up with the sleeves torn off, stares at him, chewing intently as he sticks his index finger and then his thumb into his mouth before wiping it on the front of his shirt. He seems to be enjoying his meal quite a bit as he chases the taste with a big drink from his glass. He places the glass on the table and begins to chuckle to himself. Not loud, but enough to get everyone's attention as it breaks the uncomfortable silence.

"Something funny?" the man at the head of the table questions, leaning back in his seat with his belly full, eager for the response.

"Yeah. I'm amused. We've been doin' this for a few years now… We've done everything you said, we've let you lead the way, and he still ain't here. If it ain't one excuse, it's another. When's he comin'?" the man challenges, as he sits upright, wiping the grease from his mouth and beard.

"I thought you had faith brother, you do have… faith, don't cha'?" he fires back quickly.

"Now, I'm not tryin' to question you. I'm just questioning the things you got us doing. You say he is supposed to come, and we just wanna meet him is all."

The man sits quietly, constructing his response carefully. "I understand. Tonight just wasn't the night. Something was off. Something has to be off. He should be here. We're getting closer though, I can feel it."

"Maybe he just ain't comin', maybe it's us," the man says, with a 'matter-of-fact' tone in his voice.

The man, who seems to be the leader, looks around at the others to make sure that everyone is paying attention. "Just trust me. Follow me, don't let your faith waver. We'll keep trying," he states confidently.

The man leans back and picks the meat out of his teeth with the fingernail on his pinky as he lets the conversation marinate. The others in the room continue to finish their meals and some sit there, awkwardly, finished. No one wants to be the first one to get up. The man sitting at the head of the table scans the room and takes charge by standing first and taking his plate and cup to the sink area. He walks past some of the others who watch him walk toward the sink.

He walks past a pool table. As he nears the kitchen area, he passes an island countertop that has a young blonde girl, lying on a clear, plastic paint sheet. She lies there, crystal-blue eyes wide open, mascara streaks run down her face with bruising and swelling as well. Everyone begins to stand and gather their things and the moment seems to have passed and the tension lets up.

Eight months later…

Busy hands work hurriedly, neatly folding clothes and arranging them meticulously into a gym bag on the bed. A cute, blonde girl, Olivia Rose, stands at the foot of her bed. "… And when is Mike supposed to get here, you said?" she asks.

Her boyfriend Nathan sits in an office chair, spinning slowly, as he tosses a small, colorful foam football into the air, spinning it and catching it repeatedly. "He texted me a little bit ago, on his way now. He's walking across campus," he replies with boredom weighing down his voice.

"I hope he takes his time," she says, pausing as she stands there scratching her forehead, looking around the room unsure what to do next. "Ugh! And I still need to do my hair and makeup," she hangs her head.

Nathan tosses the football at her, hitting her butt. "Babe. You just need to relax. I think you're stressing out way more about going home than you were about school."

Olivia looks up with a grin at Nathan. She picks up the football and tosses it back at him. "Don't you have anything you need to be doing?"

Nathan smacks the ball away and hops out the chair quickly and scoops Olivia off of her feet. "I can think of one thing I could be doing," he says playfully as he plants her onto the bed, leaning over her.

Olivia giggles and wraps her arms around Nathan's neck and reaches her face close to his. "Oh yeah? What's that?" she asks with a smile.

He takes a deep breath and with his eyes locked on her crystal blue eyes, he looks at her lips and back into her eyes. "You," he replies as he leans in for a kiss.

Olivia grabs Nathan's face as they make out on the bed. He climbs on top of her and his hands are all over her fit body as they start getting really into it. Her hands explore his back and shoulders as they kiss passionately. Nathan pulls away and takes his shirt off and tosses it across the dorm. Olivia sits up and pulls off her gray tank top. They make out passionately, giving into the moment as their heart rates increase more with each kiss. As Nathan begins to pull the bra strap down her shoulder, kissing her collarbone, there is a knock at the door.

Nathan sits up, onto his knees with his eyes closed and a sigh. Olivia sits upright and fixes her bra strap while adjusting herself and smiling. The knocking continues with a playful musical tapping.

"You better get that," Olivia says with a playful smile as she puts her tank top back on.

Nathan pulls Olivia close to him. "You sure we can't just make him wait out there?"

Olivia smiles big while she looks into his eyes. She kisses him really softly on the lips and pushes him away. "No, we can't."

Nathan looks at her annoyed for a second before he laughs, leans down and kisses her on the lips once more. "One second!" Nathan calls out. The knocking stops and Nathan jumps out of bed and grabs his shirt off of the office chair and he puts it on as he walks to the door.

He opens the door and is greeted cheerfully by a dark-haired man with a short, well-manicured beard, graphic t-shirt, and a bulging backpack. "What's up my dude?" Nathan jeers as their hands smack and he pulls the man in close, shoulder-to-shoulder, for a bro-hug.

"Nothing much man. Ready to hit the road. How's it going? How are you guys doing?" he asks.

"Great, come in man," Nathan insists as he steps aside.

The man sees Olivia standing beside the bed. She runs over to him. "Mike!" she says as he puts his bag down and the two hug tightly. "Gosh I've missed you. What's up?" she asks with a spark of excitement.

"I've missed you guys too," Mike says, trying to match her energy. "Man, school has been… Something else, you know, classes, lectures, essays, no time to do anything, then you do it all again for a different class." He leans his head way back, looking at the ceiling and lets out a groan.

"It's crazy to think… this is just the first semester," Nathan says, followed by a pause, "at South Carolina State," he jests in a dramatic movie trailer voice.

Mike snickers, "For sure, for sure… Hey, where's Kris at? I thought I was holding you guys up."

"I imagine he is on his way and will be here any minute," Olivia replies, as she turns to her gym bag and continues packing with a hurried pace.

"Yeah, he mentioned he had some final basketball thing with his team before the break," Nathan says.

Mike nods his head and begins to pace around the dorm. "Cool, cool." Mike grabs a photo of Olivia and Nathan that sits on her bedside in a plain white frame and he studies it. Nathan looks to have just caught her while she ran into his arms and her feet are off of the ground with the two of them smiling at each other in this candid shot. "Are you guys staying with your parents or somewhere else?"

Nathan darts a glance to Olivia. "I think we're staying at Liv's place," he says, like he is tiptoeing around the answer, waiting to be corrected.

She looks at Nathan with a smile and pauses. "…Yeah, if my parents are cool with it, I mean, we're adults and all, so…" Olivia replies.

Nathan smirks at Olivia with a sense of success.

"Awesome. I am gonna stay with a friend who just got a place for a bit. Visit my parents at some point," Mike replies.

Nathan walks to the refrigerator and grabs a bottle of beer. He looks at Mike and offers it to him while he twists off the cap to the other one. "Beer?"

"Nah, I'm good dude," Mike replies.

Nathan stares at Mike in disbelief. "Sober? …Cool," he remarks. He then twists the cap off on the second bottle and takes a big swig from one.

"No, Nate. Come on, no pregaming!" Olivia shouts.

Nathan wipes the beer from his lip with the back of his hand and tosses the empty bottle into a waste basket. "What? I'm not driving."

Olivia stares at him like a dog that stole the food from the owner's plate when they weren't looking. "You know how you get when you pregame. Maybe you should wait."

From outside, there is the sound of a car honking. Mike walks over to the window. "Hey!" he says, waving with excitement. "He's here, come on,"

Nathan goes to the window and sees their friend Kris leaning against a midnight blue Dodge Challenger with his arms crossed. "Whoa! My dude got a new ride," he says while he works on the second bottle of booze. He grabs a large duffle bag off of the floor, near the window. "Come on babe."

Olivia zips up her gym bag and is gathering her things in a rush. 'Ugh, I didn't even get to do my makeup," she says, annoyed.

Nathan kisses her on the cheek in passing, "It's okay. You're gonna be in the car most of the time anyway, …Besides, you're beautiful without it," he assures her. He throws the bag over his shoulder and walks out the front door. "Ay Mike, hold up!" he shouts.

Olivia smiles and fixes her hair. She grabs her bag and looks around before leaving for a while. As she heads out, she grabs a maroon ball cap from the coat rack and puts it on, she pulls her ponytail through the hole in the back of it and makes sure to lock the door behind her.

As Olivia gets outside the gang is altogether tossing bags into the trunk of the car. The guys are catching up as Olivia approaches. "Wow, very nice car, Kris," she says sincerely.

"Yeah, yeah, you like it? I just got it. My dad helped me get it. It's a 2022 model," Kris replies. "Let me get your bag," he says as he takes her bag from her. He places it in the trunk with everyone else's bags.

"Thanks," Olivia says.

Kris arranges the bags around a spare tire and closes the trunk. The rest of the gang gets into the car, Nathan sits in the front passenger seat while Mike and Olivia sit in the back. Kris slides into the driver seat and starts the car and the engine roars as Kris looks at everyone with a side-eyed glance for approval, pressing lightly on the gas pedal to make the motor yell.

"That's pretty sweet dude," Nathan nods, in awe of the flashiness they get to ride around in.

Kris nods with a smirk on his face. "Yeah bro, you guys wanna see how fast this baby can move?"

Everyone is ready to hit the road. Nathan turns the music up as hip hop music and the bass thumps, rattling the frame of the car. Olivia reaches her arms around the passenger seat to put her arms around Nathan very lovingly. Mike reaches forward and massages Kris' shoulders lightly, "Let's get it dude!"

The car takes off with the music bumpin' as the whole gang is together and eager to get back to their hometown to make the most of their summer break. With Olivia's dorm in the rearview and the road home underneath them, adventure, and hopefully relaxation awaits.

The group has sped through traffic on I-26 North for close to two hours now. The lanes seem to be clogging up with other motorists and things have gone from a smooth eighty-five miles per hour to a stop-and-go fifteen.

"What's up with the slow down?" Mike asks, as they slowly pass cars in the lane beside them.

Kris rolls down his tinted window and cranes his head out to look ahead. "I don't know, seems to be a complete stop in the left lane though."

"Rush hour," Nathan remarks. "What a bitch."

"Think we should try to take a different way?" Olivia asks.

"That's not a bad idea, let me see what the GPS says," Kris replies as he pulls his phone off of the dashboard and starts playing with his GPS app. "Holy shit!"

"What?" They all ask collectively.

"Says there is a wreck up ahead and the road is completely blocked off." Kris shows his phone screen to everyone and there is a map displayed with the road they're on and he zooms out to show that the road is red for over six miles.

Nathan sighs as he leans his head back. "Fuuuuck that, let's get off at the next exit."

"Are you all good with that?" Kris asks everyone.

Olivia and Mike look at each other with affirmation. "Yeah, we can use a bit more scenery," Olivia says cheerfully.

"Alright then, looks like we're getting off at," Kris squints his eyes to see the exit sign up ahead. "State Route 49 North, cool, let's roll,"

"Awesome. I hate sitting in traffic," Mike snaps.

"For sure, dude," Nathan adds.

Kris looks at his phone, "Looks like this is going to add about an hour to our drive though,"

"I'm in no hurry," Olivia responds.

"Alright then. The scenic route is fine by me,"

Kris takes the exit and they are back to cruisin' under the summer sunshine and humidity. Country roads and rich, green foliage make up a lot of the scenery. The further they get from the highway, the older the houses seem to look. The more fields they see, the fewer cars there are. Columbia feels like a different world from this part of South Carolina.

2

◇

Olivia sits in the back, quiet, as she admires the beauty of the country, away from the campus, the fancy buildings, the noise, and busy day-to-day routine that she has adapted to. She sits there, tugging at a frayed string on her jean shorts, watching fields and trees zip by. Olivia finds herself lost as she stares at the country green, listening to the soundtrack of her friends laughing and catching up. Farmland and mostly older homes make up the landscape with the occasional veggie stand or aged storefront that isn't too appealing from the road. Large, hand-painted signs are fixed onto the roadsides advertising fresh vegetables, grass-fed meats, and the less frequent sign that promises salvation.

Her thoughts of being home put an involuntary smile on her face. Nathan is going to be there with her family and everyone she loves. She spaces out, daydreaming of dinner at the table together and enjoying her life. Her younger sister beside her, elated that she is home for the summer. Her mother, at the opposite end of her father, just happy to have the whole family together again. She is sitting across the table from Nathan, admiring his handsomeness as he makes jokes with her dad, probably about sports. He looks over at her at the end of his laughter and the daydream is swept away quickly, completely jarred.

"Yeah! Let's see how fast this baby can really go!" Kris howls as he swerves wildly into the oncoming lane to go around a small sedan. Kris whips through the minimal traffic, crossing over the yellow lines on the road with no turn signals and reckless abandon. The engine screams as his lead foot sleeps on the gas pedal.

Nathan hangs out of the passenger side window with his t-shirt in his hand, screaming at a minivan in passing as he bangs on the side of the door with his shirt off waving it around. "Woooo! Let's go! Come on!"

Nathan is the walking stereotype of a high school quarterback. He is good-looking, and he knows it, he is wildly popular, and he has never said no to a good time. Nathan is the backup quarterback at SC State as a freshman walk-on, with his eye on starting for the team by the end of the season.

Kris is the enabler of this close friendship. He plays all sports and is a starting point guard for the SC State men's basketball team. Kris lays on the horn as he revs the engine beside the minivan, leaning over with his tongue out at the bewildered soccer mom in the van beside them. Kris' tank top does well of showing off his muscular arms and athlete physique. Kris is a suave guy, light skinned with dark eyes and very active on social media. He is the type to jump onto the latest viral trends, and make sure he looks good for the camera. Nathan pulls himself back into the car as Kris speeds up, cutting off the van as they take off, dangerously fast down this long and flat boring stretch of worn out country paved road.

From the backseat, "It's going to be really weird when you two grow up I bet," Olivia says, playfully.

"Yeah, I can't wait to talk to my mom at my own funeral when she finds out I died in the backseat of Kris' douche-mobile on his latest ego trip," Mike says in jest. Mike is the clear-cut more serious one in the bunch when it comes to academic studies and being practical. He is not an athlete like Kris or Nathan but enjoys working out. Mike was quite the wrestler in high school though and looks like he can still hang if he wanted to. Mike sits in the backseat, behind Kris, just happy to come along for the ride.

"Hey man, my ego trip will be the most fun you have this summer. I mean, What would you be doing right now if you weren't out with us anyway?" Kris asks.

Mike pauses with a smirk on his face, "I'd probably be calling your mom to see if she needs me to do anything around the house."

Kris grins as he stares at Mike in the rearview mirror. "Oh yeah? You talk a big game, but I bet you'd be on your computer or on Youtube streaming yourself playing video games or something."

Nathan interjects, "I wonder if Mike can show your mom how to play games and work a joystick," as he nudges Kris with his elbow.

Nathan and Mike laugh and high five. "Something is wrong with you two," says Olivia with a grin.

The laughter stops but the mood remains light. "So what are we getting into tonight?" Nathan asks.

"I'm ready to get messed up and enjoy my summer break!" Kris says as he speeds up behind a small sedan and gets right up on this car's bumper, tapping on the horn like he is playing a song.

"Watch this," Nathan says, grabbing a 44 oz foam cup half full of Mountain Dew and melted ice from Kris' cup holder. Kris crosses over into the lane beside the car and pulls up beside it.

"Nathan, stop it!" Olivia bursts, with nervous laughter. Nathan ignores her and he leans out the window and tosses the cup onto the windshield of the sedan. The sedan stops and pulls over and Kris speeds ahead, leaving a cloud of white exhaust between them and the sedan.

"You're being an asshole, Nate," Olivia says.

"I'm just having fun; relax, nobody got hurt," Nathan replies.

"Yeah, but someone could get hurt! Stop being a jerk!" Olivia demands with the tone of a mother disciplining an unruly child.

Mike and Olivia look out the back window and see a man get out of his car and he is giving them the middle finger and gesturing angrily from the middle of the road. Kris is laughing and as he fixes his eyes back to the road he is met with a horn honking and a pick up truck coming at him. He reacts quickly, "Shit! Shit! SHIT!" swerving back into the right lane. He slows to the speed limit as he takes a second to breathe and then he starts to laugh again.

"That's what I'm talkin' about baby! Ay, you know what I think we should do tonight?" Nathan questions. "We should see if Brandon and his boys want to party. He's got the pool and all that."

Kris looks over at Nathan "Yeah man, I'm sure he can get some girls to come through too."

Mike leans forward between Nathan and Kris, with a dramatic pause, "But first we need beer, maybe a little weed."

Olivia rolls her eyes. "It's gonna be dark soon, we should figure it out now. I'm not sure how much longer I can sit in this car while Kris tries to get us killed."

"Tell me you don't feel alive when we hang out though?" Kris asks, in a jovial tone.

"Alright. Let's stop and grab beer and some snacks at the next gas station first, and then we will head to Brandon's crib," Nathan suggests.

"Sounds like a plan to me!" Kris replies, as he turns the music up. 'Shout at the Devil' by Motley Crue plays at an obnoxious volume. "Hey… Check this out," Kris remarks. "That's one rinky-dink church van."

Kris slows to match the van's speed, riding close to the bumper. This is an older transit van, painted white and chipping with blue hand-painted letters on the side "Glenn Springs House of God" and underneath it "A traditional, faith based community." On the back of the van, in red letters it reads on the left door "Hell is REAL" and on the right door in blue letters "And so is HE."

"These hillbilly churches have always creeped me out," Olivia adds.

"Well maybe we can creep them out," Nate says, as he rolls the window down. He climbs out of the window and sits on the door, hanging onto the inside with his shirt off and starts twirling it against the wind, screaming. "Woooooo! Turn that shit up!" Kris pulls into the other lane and speeds up alongside the van and turns the music up louder. Nathan shouts the words to the chorus as he makes faces at the people inside of the van, who seem very unamused. The van is all older people from what he can tell. Nathan reaches out and knocks on the glass and the man in the window seat turns to him and gives a look of annoyance, shaking his head in disapproval as he looks away. Nathan begins to tap on the glass harder and is singing the words even louder and more obnoxiously. He sees the lack of amusement and he climbs back into the car.

"Watch this," Kris says as he practically puts his foot through the floor mashing it against the gas pedal.

Olivia shoots a look over at Mike and they have an unspoken, mutual concern at the way Kris and Nathan are acting right now. "Guys. Okay. Knock it off now!" Olivia urges. "These people aren't scared and you're going to hurt yourselves or all of us. This really isn't safe," she adds.

"Yeah, guys. Put your dicks away and let's just go. Fuck this van," Mike adds.

Kris speeds up and cuts the van off and then slams on the brakes, causing the bus to swerve to avoid rear ending them. Brake checked! Kris and Nathan burst into laughter. Olivia and Mike clench anything they can in the backseat. Olivia leans forward and smacks Kris several times, "You fucking asshole!" Kris continues to laugh, pleased with his behavior.

"Fuck yeah. Let's go!" Nathan cheers.

"That was so uncool dude," Mike expresses to the guys in the front, completely stone-faced. Mike loosens up his grip on the inside door handle and lets out an audible exhale "Fuck guys, is that the gas station up ahead on the right? Pull in real quick. I think I need to change my underwear."

"Lighten up dude. You're about to be faded in no time," Nathan responds through an elated grin.

Olivia looks at her phone and sees that she has notifications but no signal so she isn't able to view anything. "How far is Brandon from where we are?"

"Few miles or so. I'm not entirely sure where we are honestly," Nathan adds.

"Bro, I thought you knew where we were at," Kris huffed.

"Dude, you're the one driving!" Nathan replies.

"Guys, are you serious?" Olivia asks.

"Just Google the nearest highway real quick," Nathan answers.

Olivia looks at Nathan with annoyance washed over her face. "I don't have a signal, or I would, Captain Obvious,"

Mike looks at his phone, "Yeah, I don't have any bars either. Just pull in and we can ask the cashier maybe where the nearest highway is."

The band of eager-to-party college students pull into the gravel lot of this gas station. It looks like it used to be an old BP gas station that the company forgot about, and the owners of the convenience store just started making it their own. The sign near the road is green but looks like the sun has really had its way with the color and stripped it of its vibrance. There is a reader board with yellowed and kind of old-looking, and cracked letters that says "COLD BE R." One of the letters is missing and the "R" looks like it might fall at the slightest breeze. There are only two gas pumps in the lot. Describing this place as unorthodox would be an understatement.

The building is small. There is an icebox outside with a rusted chain and lock. The windows and the glass on the door look foggy and in desperate need of moisture and a rag. An old vending machine sits outside of the door, humming away with a flickering bulb. Looking at this place from the outside would give any normal person the urge to wash their hands. Looking at this place for too long was the equivalent of watching someone sneeze into a handkerchief and then wipe their mouth and put it back into their pocket.

There is a dirt road that goes around the back of the gas station and it leads to a big barn that can be seen from the street. Dozens of junked cars and other vehicles are littered along the side of the lot, along the grass and shrubs. Some look like they need work… some more than others.

Kris parks at one of the pumps and everyone gets out of the car. As they're walking toward the entrance they hear someone pull into the lot. It's the van from the road, parking on the other side of the pump. Nathan nudges Mike "Yo, check it out. These people are old as hell. They look like they're about to die any second," he says with amusement.

Olivia speaks up. "Guys, leave them alone already."

"I'm just fuckin' around babe, chill," Nathan says as he laughs it off.

Kris begins to walk slowly and hunches over as if he is old, groaning like he is an elderly person. "Here, let me get the door honey… Oh! Ouch! I hurt myself!"

Olivia gasps, unamused and a little embarrassed. "Knock it off, that's so mean, they're probably really nice people," she stammers. The group has a laugh about it as Kris holds open the door for everyone.

They all proceed into the convenience store with a destination in mind, and an appetite for beer and snacks before they continue their journey.

3

◇

Mike is a man on a mission heading straight to the freezers to look at the beer selection. Nathan is right behind him, with a head start to a nice buzz. Kris is grabbing snacks like it's a contest to grab as much as you can in the littlest amount of time.

Olivia is taking a look around when the cashier nods and greets her. "Howdy miss. Real scorcher out there today, yeah?" he asks, as he uses the front of his shirt to wipe sweat off of his face.

Olivia smiles politely, "Yeah, one of those days where you appreciate air conditioning."

The cashier leans onto the counter and smiles real big, showing off an aged smile paired with nearly blackened gums. "Yeah, but who needs AC when lookin' at you gives me chills, honey."

Olivia fights back the look of disgust she is certainly feeling at this moment and says nothing. She paces around the counter to avoid any more interaction with this dirty and flirty cashier.

Mike and Nathan grab several cases of beer and are barreling toward the counter. Olivia is looking at a sunglasses rack and trying them on in the dirty mirror as she waits. She switches to another pair and looks in the mirror, and then another when a bell dings at the front door. She sees three older gentlemen and an older woman walk into the shop through the reflection.

"How goes it Ozzy?" the cashier asks cheerfully.

"Well, it's going. How you doin' Bobby?" Ozzy groans. Ozzy is an older man. Salt and peppered-hair, dark goatee with hints of white in it as well. He is not an imposing figure at all but looks physically fit. He is dressed the best of everyone that walked in with him, wearing a collared shirt tucked into his blue jeans, sleeves rolled up, and a silver watch to complete the look.

The conversation continues and Olivia is watching the other guys who came in along with the woman. Olivia gets lost in this reflection, daydreaming, when the woman looks up and makes eye contact in the reflection. Olivia nervously looks away and acts as if she wasn't just staring at the people who walked in. She looks intently at the glasses she's holding them while passively listening to the conversations around her. Nathan and Mike are making small talk with the cashier as Ozzy and the other fellas are behind them in line. Olivia is focused on the glasses, listening, and as she turns, the woman is standing there. "Shit!" Olivia gasps and drops the glasses onto the floor.

"You know, your friend should really be a little more considerate on the road," the woman warns, with a scowl on her pale face. Her lips, pink. She wears her light brown hair, with shades of gray down, about shoulder length. She's wearing jeans and a button-up flannel shirt with her sleeves rolled up tight, past her elbows, and work boots. Everything about this woman's look screams "painfully ordinary" considering the setting.

"I'm so sorry. I didn't mean–" Olivia says as she almost runs into her.

"Y'alls not from round here, are ya?" the woman interrupts.

Olivia fumbles over her words nervously and starts to put the glasses back onto the hooks, clearly a little uncomfortable. "Us? No, well yes, but we're here on–"

The woman interrupts once more, "The ones with the blue lenses."

"I'm sorry?" Olivia replies, looking a little confused

"The blue ones honey. You should get the blue ones. They look good on you. I think your hair is really pretty too," the woman continues, maintaining eye contact.

Olivia puts the glasses back on the hook, in a rush. "Thank you… I don't really need these though… Listen, I'm sorry about my friends. They're just a little… Rambunctious. You know, with school being out and all."

The woman watches Olivia fumble putting the glasses back. "Well… You kids just stay outta trouble, ya hear?" Olivia smiles at the woman with one of those uncomfortable smiles you give someone when you're just being polite, but the smile isn't necessarily a happy one. Olivia walks over to the counter and stands beside Nathan.

Nathan and Mike are engaged in a discussion with the cashier about South Carolina State football and how they could be better than North Carolina University. One of the men behind them in line joins the conversation. An older gentleman with a scruffy beard that rests on a farmer's tan and weathered face. He wears a well-loved, albeit dingy, flannel shirt with the sleeves torn off and a dirty Texas Longhorns hat with small tears on the bill of the hat. "SC ain't nothin' but a bunch of entitled yuppies, too scared to get hit," he says, self-assured.

Nathan turns back to the old man, offended. "What's that old-timer?"

The old man looks Nathan up and down. "I think you heard me, son."

Nathan steps up to the man with an attitude. "You're talking to South Carolina's future, the next quarterback. Ain't nobody scared to take a hit on my team. I don't know who you're watching."

The man laughs, and looks at his buddies. "Hmmph, maybe you'd be better off going to a real school then, youngin'."

Nathan begins to raise his voice. "Who you callin' youngin'?"

Mike steps in front of Nathan and the old man. "Come on Nate, chill"

"Yeah Nate, listen to your sissy friend, and chill." the man antagonizes.

Kris sets his arms full of junk food down onto the nearest shelf and rushes over to what might become an altercation. One of the other men stands between Kris and his friends and puts his hand against Kris' chest. The cashier speaks out. "Guys, let's not do this in here–"

Mike then steps toward the man dishing out insults. "What did you just say?"

Ozzy steps in front of the old man, while side eyeing Nathan and Mike. Ozzy looks at the man, standing face to face with Nathan. "Come on' Cliff. Let's just calm down. Let's let these folks go on about their night."

Cliff looks at Ozzy, upset. He pulls the hat off his head and smacks it across his thigh, puts his hands on his waist, frustrated, looking at the cashier as if to receive validation of some sort. "These are the same motherfuckers from the road Oz!"

Ozzy looks at Cliff with a patient tone. "I know, I know. It's alright."

Cliff takes a deep breath and sighs. He throws his hands up, "Fine, whatever," he growls as he storms out the door.

Olivia grabs Nathan by the arm. "Come on. Let's just go," she suggests.

Nathan is fuming, with his face red, he turns to the cashier and grabs the cases of beer.

Mike grabs the rest of the stuff on the counter and looks at the cashier. "Have a good night."

Kris pushes the old man's hand off of his chest and follows everyone out of the store.

The group of friends charge out of the convenience store with the beer secured, hustling back to the car. Nathan is visibly angry as Olivia tries to keep up with his hurried pace. "Nathan!" Olivia shouts at his back, to no reaction. "Nathan! Hold up a second, would you?" she says reaching for his arm, as she is almost jogging to match his pace.

There is another man standing outside of the van, wearing a stained shirt, and matted hair, staring at Kris' car, and he sees Nathan, looking him up and down. "Evenin' folks. Everything alright?"

Nathan, with his eyes focused on the passenger side door, not looking at the man at all, opens the door. "Go to Hell," he mutters, climbing into the car as he slams the door.

Olivia looks at the man, clearly embarrassed by Nathan's behavior, she opens the rear passenger side door and looks at the man, "I'm sorry about that. Now is not a good time."

Mike and Kris walk around to the driver side and as Kris is opening the driver side door, the man at the gas pump looks at Kris, "That's a fuckin' sweet ride brother!" Kris makes eye contact, still seething from the altercation inside, but doesn't say anything back. "Yeah I always wanted me one of these newer Dodge Challengers. They got some serious power under the hood huh?" the old man continues, as he stands in awe of the vehicle. Kris gets into the car and shuts the door. All of the windows come down as Kris starts the vehicle and the motor roars. The old man steps near the car with a grin and spits onto the ground, nodding his head to the music that the engine is conducting, "Oh yeah, yeah buddy that is some serious noise. I love that shit right there!" Kris, without even acknowledging the man's adoration drives off, kicking up dust and speeding off into the road. As they are driving off, Mike and Olivia are looking back and see the three men and the woman walk out of the shop and to the van. They are all staring at them as they drive away. "Well that was… eventful, huh?" Mike poked, trying to lighten the mood.

"Motherfucking rednecks! That dude is lucky I didn't knock his ass out," Nathan fumes.

Olivia leans forward and puts her hand on Nathan's shoulder and rubs his chest. "It's alright. It's over. Now we can go have some fun," she assured.

"Where should we be headed?" Kris asks through a glass stare of frustration.

"Fuck!" Nathan says under his breath. "All that shit happened back there and I didn't ask the cashier where the highway was."

"It's cool," Kris replies, "I'll just drive until something looks familiar."

Nathan sighs and stares out the window quietly. The road is straight for as far as you can see ahead. Fields, pastures, and farmland on all sides with the occasional house. Truly, the middle of nowhere.

They drive away from the gas station and get a few miles down the road when the car begins to shake. "What the –" Kris wondered aloud.

Olivia leans forward with concern. "What's going on?"

Kris groans, aggravated. "I think we might have a flat."

"Do you have a spare bro?" Mike asks quickly.

"Yeah, I do." Kris answers as he pulls to the side of the road. There is nothing around them other than fields and tall stalks of corn, wheat, and sunflowers. The area is flat with nothing much to be seen in the distance from all sides. Kris gets out of the car and looks at the wheels. The rear driver side tire is completely flat and looks like the tire was torn apart. "Fuck!" Kris shouts. Everyone else gets out of the car to see what is going on.

"Oh… wow, that's not good," Mike says. Kris has his hands on his head and is clearly frustrated. Mike slaps the trunk of the car. "Pop the trunk man. I will put the spare on." Kris grabs his keys and pushes the button to open the trunk. Mike walks over to the trunk and sees everyone's bags, but they look like they have been rummaged through now. Mike moves the bags around and sees a loose tire jack with no spare tire. Mike turns to Kris. "Hey bro. Your spare is missing."

Kris walks to the trunk. He sees his bag open "Dude. Why the fuck is my shit opened and like that?"

Mike stares at Kris puzzled. "That's how it was when I opened the trunk dude. It looks like all of our stuff is like that."

"How did all of our stuff get opened? Is anything missing?" Nathan asks as he shuffles through his loose clothes that are scattered about the trunk.

"That is really weird. I know I saw a wheel in the trunk when we left the dorm," Olivia adds.

"See!" Kris reacts to her comment feeling validated. Baffled, his voice raises with agitation, "I know there was a tire in there. This is practically a brand new car."

Mike watches Kris throw a fit and pauses awkwardly. "What are we gonna do?"

Olivia and Nathan both check their phones. Nathan shows Olivia his phone. "I still don't have a signal."

Olivia looks at her phone. "Yeah, neither do I."

Kris looks at everyone for a moment. This inconvenience has put a damper on the evening as he has an outburst and kicks the rear bumper. "FUCK!

4

◇

"So, what are we going to do now?" Olivia asks.

"I really don't know." Kris replies, as he looks at his phone while also having no signal. "Shit."

Mike closes the trunk. "Maybe we can wave someone down and they can help us."

Kris stares at Mike. "We don't know how long that will take though."

Olivia is looking up the road, and turns around to look back the way they came from. "It's going to be dark soon. I don't think we should be out here." The group stands around quietly, fishing for pieces of a plan for a moment.

"We aren't going to fix this problem just standing here like a bunch of sitting ducks," Nathan barks at the group.

"What do you suggest we do then?" Mike fires back.

"Two of us can walk back up the road to the gas station, ask the cashier to use the phone," Nathan suggests.

"You really think that's a good idea, after the way we left?" Kris questions.

"I mean, I'm not too proud to apologize on behalf of the group if there is a need for it," Mike offers hesitantly.

Nathan pulls out his wallet and grabs a crisp twenty dollar bill. "Fuck. Well, maybe money talks with this guy."

Kris looks over at Olivia. "Maybe Liv can go and turn the charm on with the cashier."

Nathan backhands Kris' chest. "Dude, what the fuck?"

Kris grins. "What? I saw the way he was shootin' his shot with you back there."

Olivia wears a look of disgust. "Ew. No. And fuck you for thinking that is even an option."

Mike opens a can of beer, takes a drink and leans against the car. "Well …The alternative is to sit out here all night and drink under the stars."

Nathan sighs. "Who wants to walk up there with me?" No one replies as they all look at each other anticipating someone to speak up. "Seriously? No one?"

Kris tosses Mike the keys. "Fuck it… I'll go."

Nathan claps his hands together in excitement, but mostly relief. "Alright! That's my boy," Nathan walks over to Olivia and leans in for a kiss. "I'll be back soon, baby."

Olivia hugs him tight. She grabs his chin and makes him look at her. "Don't say anything stupid please. I really don't want to be out here all night."

Kris looks at Olivia, "We won't be too long. Don't worry."

Kris and Nathan begin walking back to the gas station with a little pep in their step. Olivia leans on the car. Mike sits on the trunk of the car dangling his feet. There is a long pause between the two.

Mike leans back and rests against the back window. "It's quiet out here… So quiet that it's almost loud in a way," he says to Olivia.

Olivia admires the sky, taking in the silence on all sides of them. No cars, no people to be heard or seen. Just tall grass, trees, and the two lane road that is worn from years of sun and weather. "At least the sunset is pretty," she quips.

"What are we gonna do if they aren't back soon?" Mike asks.

"I really don't know what we can do. I guess wait in the car." Olivia says.

"So, like camping," Mike responds with a snicker and a smile.

Olivia laughs, "Yeah, camping, you can say that." Olivia slumps down the side of the car and sits on the ground, facing the street. She plays with her phone but doesn't have service so it is basically a glorified flashlight. She also notices her battery is getting low. The silence ensues as the orange sky becomes a pale blue, and then a blanket of darkness. There are more stars in the sky than you would see if you were in the city. Silhouettes of the distant treelines clash with the horizon during sunset. Black bleeding into the purple-ish/deep blue of the night sky. The moon watches them from the deep, dark sky, as they wait for the next motorist to use this worn road.

Olivia and Mike perk up when they see headlights approaching in the distance. At least forty minutes have passed since Kris and Nathan started walking.

Mike hops off of the car, to his feet and looks over at Olivia "Think we should try to stop them?"

"This is the first car we've seen in a while," she says.

Mike steps out to the road and begins waving his arms to flag the car down. As the car approaches, Olivia also walks toward the road waving the same as Mike is doing. The car honks their horn a few times and then speeds right past the two.

"God dammit!" Mike says as he drops his arms in defeat.

"It's fine," Olivia says. "Kris and Nate should be back soon."

Olivia lays on the hood of the car. Mike leans against the front as they go back to waiting anxiously. Olivia hears the caw of a black crow nearby. She looks in the direction of it and sees it perched on a nearby road sign, like a bad omen. Olivia takes a deep breath and sighs as she tries to shake the uneasy feeling that has come over her. She sits up and looks at Mike "Hey, Mike."

"Yeah?" he replies.

"What's your plan? …You know, after school and stuff?"

Mike pauses for a moment. "Hmm. Well, I am really just wanting to get through school, and then start looking for a job somewhere new. Maybe something with video games or something. I feel like I've been tied to this town for too long. That was one of the major reasons I went to a school a little further away, so I can just adapt to not being here."

"Oh, I always thought you went there so you could stay close to Kris and Nathan," Olivia comments as she fiddles with her phone, spinning it in her hands, listening.

"It was one reason I went, but I think once everyone is finished with school, we're all going to go on about our grown up lives, and we'll say we will see each other, and hang out… but I know people will have kids, or get too busy. That's just how these things go, ya know? No sense in sticking around and regretting it." Mike pauses for a moment.

Olivia looks at him. "I get it. But you know, we're all always going to be friends. But I guess you're right. I watched my parents and family do that same thing you just described."

Mike looks at Olivia, "How bout' you, what's your plan?"

Olivia shrugs. "I guess I don't have much of a plan, yet. I've been so focused on school, school, school, that I guess I just hoped it would fall into place along the way. Then Nathan and I started dating, and all of a sudden it's serious, but I still don't know how serious he thinks it is."

Mike snickers. "You should definitely have that discussion with him sooner rather than later."

"Maybe before we go back next semester," she says in an upbeat tone.

Mike looks at Olivia very straight-faced before he cracks a soft grin. "I know one thing… Nathan is probably one of the most driven people I know. I could never tell him that though because his head would swell up. But you and him… I see how he looks at you. He is all in when it comes to you. I think he really loves you."

Olivia stares at Mike and smiles. "I definitely love him too." Olivia blurts out through a laugh. "Like, a lot… I'm crazy about him."

Mike stares at her grinning. "Nathan is one of my oldest friends. I remember girls he would have crushes on back in grade school. Then girls he dated early in high school. He never looked at them or talked about them the way he does with you."

Olivia laughs. "Were there many others?"

Mike shakes his head with a bigger smile and joy in his voice. "There were a few. That's all I will say."

Olivia laughs it off. "Fine, I will take that, I guess."

Mike looks out to the night sky and exhales after laughing. "He is just one of the more focused guys I've ever been around. Determined. When we were in high school, his grades were C's and D's on a good day, but he wanted to be the starting quarterback. He had to get his grades straight in all classes to be able to play though. He was so driven to play and get a scholarship that in just one semester he started staying later, got a tutor, and in no time was an A-B student. He set a goal, got tunnel vision and made it happen. I always wished I were more like him in that way. Nathan …Now Nathan is a man with a plan."

Olivia smiles harder. "I guess we better step it up on our end then."

Mike leans his head out to look down the road. "Maybe… Oh! Hey! There's another car coming from that way."

In the other direction there is another set of headlights approaching. Olivia and Mike both walk toward the road and begin to wave their arms. The vehicle comes closer and the lights are almost blinding. It begins to slow down and passes the two and pulls over to the shoulder in front of the broken down Dodge Challenger. It is an older pickup truck. Blue, in need of some tender love and care. Paint would go a long way with this truck. There is a tow pulley mounted to the truck bed. The engine shuts off and the driver side door opens. An older man steps out and slams the door shut. The man walks toward Mike and Olivia wearing a dirty navy blue military hat with the yellow embroidered letters saying "Vietnam" accompanied by the service ribbon, a plain navy t-shirt, with a pack of cigarettes and glasses in his front shirt pocket. His shirt tucked in, with dirty jeans and suspenders, and a big shining belt buckle. His face weathered, intense eyes, beard long and unkept, and a cigarette teetering off of his lips in the corner of his mouth.

"Y'all needin' some help, it's lookin' like," the man observes.

Mike walks toward the man. "Hello, sir. Thanks for stopping. We had a tire blow out and didn't have a spare. This is our friend's car and he and another friend walked up to the gas station back that way, a couple hours ago to use the phone. We don't have any service on our phones."

The man walks over to the blown out tire. "Hmmmph." The man crouches down and looks closely at the wheel. "Looks like this rim has been beat to shit… Welp, there ain't no sense in you two sittin' out here all night… Here's what I can do." Mike and Olivia stand alongside the man at full attention. "I live just up the road-a-ways, I can attach you to the wrecker I got here and we head down. I have a garage, I can try to fix you up and get you on your way. Whaddaya say?"

Olivia looks to Mike, "What about Kris and Nate?"

Mike turns to Olivia for a sidebar conversation, "The guys have been gone a while already. What if we leave a note telling them we will be back or something?"

Olivia looks disgusted at Mike. "A note! You would leave them out here all night, not sure where we're at, after they just walked all the way back?"

"Well, I really don't know what to do here." Mike replies.

"Might I offer a suggestion?" the old man intervenes. "We do as I said before, and we can head to my house. I got the garage. And I can have my wife drive up the road to see if your friends are at the gas station or walkin' along the road. If she sees them, she can pick them up, and bring them to you. Easy peasy, problem solved."

Mike looks at Olivia. "Look, I don't like it anymore than you, but do you have a better suggestion?"

Olivia begrudgingly agrees. She is uneasy about the decision and has a terrible feeling in her gut. She steps out onto the road and hopes she sees Kris and Nathan walking back before they leave. She looks at her phone once more to make sure she doesn't magically have a signal, and still nothing.

"Alrighty then. I'll hook 'err on up and we can get going." the old man says. "The name is Virgil by the way. Friends call me Wild Turkey," he grins as he walks to the bed of his truck.

Mike extends his hand, "I'm Mike, this is Olivia."

Virgil puts his cigarette out on the side of the truck and throws the butt onto the ground before shaking Mike's hand. "It's nice to meet yas," he grumbles as he starts to unravel some chains from the truck.

Mike goes to Olivia to offer comfort. "You see, it's all going to be fine. We're going to get this fixed. I'm sure he has a phone there, or Wi-Fi or something. His wife is going to go pick up the guys, all is safe, and all is–" *THWACK!* Mike falls to the ground like a bag of gravel and Virgil stands behind him with the chain dangling from his hand, and the heavy tow hook on the end, swinging at his feet.

"MIKE! Oh my god! Mike!" Olivia screams and she quickly becomes frantic. Virgil steps over Mike's body and toward Olivia with the chain in hand and she is frozen, in disbelief. Stricken with fear, this cannot be real, she thinks. Virgil reaches for Olivia and she jerks away. She tries to run but is stumbling around, confused. "Help me! Please! No!" she cries aloud, fighting Virgil's hand away as he tries to grab her.

"Now come on missy, stop strugglin' already, and make this easier on the both of us!" Virgil commands as he manages to grab one of her arms while she is flailing wildly. She begins to kick at him, desperate to escape. She punches him in the face several times before he reaches back and backhands her so hard he lets her go and they both fall to the ground. Virgil gets back to his feet first and he walks to Olivia who is slow to get up. He picks up the chain and reaches down, pulling Olivia to her feet quickly. He begins to wrap her tight in the chains and he leaves her on the ground, bounded and restrained.

Mike opens his eyes and raises his head slowly, with pain on his face, and dizziness as he tries to focus. He touches the back of his head and looks at his hand to see blood. "Ow! Fuuuuuck! Ahhh!" Mike crawls, trying to get to his feet and he sees Olivia in the chains. Virgil is now leaning into the driver side of his truck. Mike is having a difficult time getting to his feet, and not even sure what has happened in this short time. "Olivia!" he calls out.

Virgil looks over at Mike. "Well, well, we got us a tough guy don't we?" Virgil, with a roll of twine in hand, walks over and presses his boot to Mike's back, a firm suggestion that he lay still. Virgil drops to one knee and puts one of Mike's hands behind his back, tying it up at the wrist, followed by the other hand. He then drags Mike to the rear of the pick up truck and hoists him up into the bed. "Hrrrrpppphmm!" He drops Mike into the bed of the truck. He grabs a shop rag that is already filthy with stains on it that is laying in the bed of the truck, and he stuffs it into Mike's mouth. Virgil stands there and wipes the sweat from his forehead. "Let me tell ya, I'm no spring chicken anymore," as he smiles. Virgil then grabs Olivia and tosses her into the front seat of his truck. He uses more twine to secure her wrists together and ankles as well.

Virgil looks at Olivia and touches her face. He grabs her chin and turns her head to the left, and then the right, as she stares at him from the corner of her eye, heart-pounding and breathing heavily through her nose. He sees her phone in her back pocket and he pulls it out and tosses it onto the dashboard. He caresses her face gently more as he stares at her. "Well, I think you're gonna do just fine sweetheart… They are just going to love you," Virgil says aloud, as she looks at him in absolute wide-eyed horror. Virgil shuts the door and walks to the Dodge Challenger and begins to hum an old Johnny Cash song. As he is singing, he is gathering more chains and now hooking up the car to his wrecker. He is humming the song as he raises the car and is ready to go. He walks over to the driver door, still humming, opens the door, gets in, starts the engine and begins to drive away as his humming turns into singing. In the seat beside him, is a walkie talkie. Virgil's singing is disrupted by a call.

"Homebase to Wild Turkey, got a copy? Over."

5

◇

Earlier that evening....

Kris and Nathan are walking up the road, several miles behind them in the humid country heat. The night sky completely suffocates everything they can see in all directions, with exception to the gas station sign on the side of the road that is off in the distance. The lights in the old reader board flicker dimly with a warm, dull glow, and have a bulb or two out from the looks of things. Where it normally reads "COLD BE R", it just looks like "COLD" now, with the bad lighting.

Nathan points ahead. "There it is. Almost there."

"Uh huh," Kris mutters, not offering up much of a response.

"I think I might just head home after this. This kind of put a damper on the whole night dude. We might have to get together another day," Nathan offered with his pregame buzz completely dead now.

Kris looks over at Nathan with a straight face. "You sure man? I feel like we should be able to get this fixed tonight. Just a bump in the road is all."

Nathan looks ahead with pause. Trudging along at a militant pace, "Yeah… I just know that when we get back to the car, Olivia is probably gonna be tired, and annoyed about this all. I'm just not feeling much up for a party now."

Kris nods his head in understanding. "This doesn't have anything to do with that guy from earlier getting in your face does it?"

"I don't know. I'm just thinking, maybe I was being an ass. I'm just not feelin' it now," Nathan explains with a change in energy.

Kris sighs in defeat. "Ight, that's cool."

The guys approach the gas station and just as they are walking up, the cashier appears to be coming outside, and he is locking up the front door. Kris begins to jog up to try and catch him before he walks away.

"Excuse me!" Kris shouts from across the lot. The cashier stops, and waits. "Hi," Kris calls out, slightly winded and breathing heavily.

"You boys are about five minutes too late, I'm all closed up for the night," the cashier says regretfully.

"No, no, we just need to use a telephone," Kris clarified.

"You boys in some sorta trouble or somethin'?" the cashier asks.

Nathan looks at the man as he starts to walk away. "Listen, Bobby… It was Bobby, right?"

Bobby stops and looks at Nathan. "Yeah."

"Look Bobby, we were here a couple hours ago–" Nathan starts.

Bobby interrupts, "Oh I remember. You guys stirred up quite a pot of shit."

Nathan looks at Kris and then back to Bobby. "Yeah… Listen. That was all me, man. I came in, I was just being a little wild. I let my emotions get the better of me. I apologize."

Bobby giggles, "Well, I don't think I'm the one you need to be apologizing to, quite frankly."

Uncomfortably, Kris sighs. "Sir, we just need to use a phone. Five minutes, tops! And we're gone. Please."

Bobby stands there for a moment, eyeballing the two, with his keys in his hand. Just as he takes a deep breath to speak, a voice comes from around the corner of the building.

"You boys need help with something?" One of the guys from the altercation in the gas station earlier walks into the conversation. The man has long gray/white/black hair, but mostly gray, a whiskey stained mustache, with a grizzly face. A dirty t-shirt underneath a jean jacket with the sleeves cut off. He has rings on his fingers, tattoos that look homemade all up his arms, a necklace with a cross on it, worn-out jeans, and well-aged work-boots.

"Bobby, why don't you go ahead and take off buddy. I'll see if I can help our wayward friends here."

Bobby walks away, without any hesitation, and heads toward an old station wagon parked at the outside of the lot, close to the road. "Well alright then, you boys take care now."

The man looks at Kris, then over to Nathan and smirks. He gives a light laugh to himself. "Name's Jasper. I believe we met earlier today just inside there. Not really *met, met,* but you know what I'm sayin'."

Nathan swallows his pride and speaks up, "I'm sorry about what happened, and how I–"

Jasper interrupts in a peaceful, cool sort of tone. "Son, son… Water under the bridge." As he moves his hands in the motion of a baseball umpire calling "safe" at home plate.

Kris responds, "We didn't mean any disrespect earlier. We were just–"

Jasper interrupts, again. "Listen, it's okay. I was young once too. I got into my fair share of shit in my day, still do, from time to time contrary to what you two rascals might think."

Kris looks at Nathan, a little confused, and more uncomfortable. "Sir–"

Jasper interrupts Kris, "Please. Call me Jasper. My father was sir."

Kris pauses. "…Jasper, …We had a tire blow out a couple miles up the road as we were leaving here."

"Well ain't that a shame, "Jasper says with a playfully sarcastic tone.

"Yeah. We walked all the way back here hoping to use the phone to call a friend or something," Kris explains.

"Well ain'tcha got a spare?" Jasper asks, smiling like a serpent.

"Actually, I did have a spare, but it's gone now," Kris says, annoyed.

Jasper looks at Kris. "Hmmph…"

Jasper pulls a pack of cigarettes with a shiny zippo out from his vest pocket. He takes a cigarette from the pack with his lips, opens the zippo, and strikes it against his leg to fire it up, and lights his cigarette, closes the lighter, and inhales deeply as he puts it away. He blows a big cloud of smoke into the wind.

"So you got a spare… But you ain't got no spare?" Jasper asks, with a puzzled expression.

Kris responds, a little frustrated, "I- I had a spare, I know I did–"

Nathan interjects, "There is no spare tire, is the point here. We just need a spare or a phone."

Jasper looks at the boys, takes another deep drag of his cigarette. "Well I'll tell you what," Jasper blows a big cloud of smoke into the air. "Why don't we take a walk back here, you see this big barn back there? You boys can make your phone calls, and cool off or whatever, and I will drive you back to your car if you'd like."

Nathan perks up a bit. "Really? Even after the way I acted earlier?" Kris has a look of uncertainty and is a little suspicious of Jasper.

"Now I understand you were just being a little shit. But let's look at the brighter side… Nobody got hurt. Now you need a break, it seems and we're in a position to do something good, and I think we all can use a little good karma, am I right?" Jasper says to the two, with a look of reassurance.

Nathan looks at Kris, and then back to Jasper. "Thank you Jasper. We appreciate it."

"Well alright then. Follow me." Jasper leads.

Kris stands still. "I'm sorry, I just want to make sure. Is there some kind of catch to this? We harass you on the road, almost get into a fight in the gas station, and now you're going to help us?"

Nathan slaps Kris' chest and gives him a wide eyed look and motions his mouth to say 'shut up.'

"It's just a little weird to me, is all." Kris protests.

Jasper tosses his cigarette onto the ground and snuffs it out with his boot. He then walks over to Kris with a bit more aggressive body language now.

"If someone is starving, and a good samaritan comes along and offers bread, that person that's starving isn't gonna ask how it's seasoned. I know you saw the writing on that van earlier. This is a church young man. A CHURCH!" Jasper is in Kris' face now poking his chest, as it appears all of the questions have struck a chord with Jasper in this offering of charity. "We are righteous people. We are offering you what you need. We aren't asking for anything in return. You need bread, I have bread. Take the goddamn bread!"

Nathan steps in between Kris and Jasper, as Jasper is becoming a little irate toward Kris after his intentions were put under the looking glass. "Jasper. I apologize for my friend here. It's been a long day. It's hot out here. It's dark, and we just want to get back to our friends and get home as soon as possible. I'm sure Kris didn't mean any disrespect sir."

Jasper turns sternly to Nathan. "I said, it's Jasper!" he hisses.

"…Right …Jasper. I'm sorry," Nathan corrects, as he is now playing damage control and mediating this interaction. "Let's start over." Nathan takes a deep breath. "May we please use your phone, Jasper?"

Jasper stares at Kris with a scowl on his face, then smiles wide and turns to Nathan. "Sure, son. It would be ungodly not to lend a helping hand."

6

◇

Kris and Nathan follow behind Jasper to the barn that sits behind the gas station. Looking around the area, there is a lot going on. There are, most noticeably, rows of cars. There are some older cars, newer cars, a few really nice luxury cars that have been scrapped and pieced out. The majority of cars are beat up. Some look like they've been in wrecks. Others have the doors torn off, some completely smashed to hell. Others have mirrors missing, headlights and tail lights busted, windshields busted up, a few are even stacked on top of each other, tires and wheels stacked like retaining walls in some areas. There is a shed behind the barn that can be faintly seen from the front lot. There are a few different spots that look like fire pits. Picnic tables are peppered throughout the lot. There is a big tractor beside the barn. It's old and looks like it's not been driven in a while.

Kris looks around, still suspicious of Jasper and this area. Nathan follows along, not far behind Jasper. "So what kind of church is this?" Nathan asks.

"Well, it's more of a community church. Folks from all over the county come here. Most of 'em locals. Been comin' here for years too," Jasper replies.

"What kind of people come to this church?" Nathan asks.

"Oh, you know… Anybody that's anybody." Jasper rasps.

Nathan looks over to Kris and they both look a little concerned at the lack of an actual answer. As they approach the barn, they see the white van from the road, parked. The barn doors open wide, and the light inside shines out into the lot. A couple of guys walk out and start igniting paper and tossing it into old barrels that they use for bonfires. They seem to be preparing for some sort of ceremony or party.

"Hey Jasper! We're about to be set up, whenever you're ready, brother," a woman says to him at the door.

"Thanks darlin'," he says back with a smirk and a wink.

"Jasper. Ozzy is waitin' on ya," another woman says.

"Let 'em know I'm in the hall and have *guests* please, would ya?" he responds as he leans close to her and looks at her like there is an inside joke or something.

"Right away brother," she replies as she scurries off, quickly.

They walk into the barn and it is very lively. Things are much more organized and clean inside, despite the outside. There are at least twenty people here, maybe thirty, all older people. It seems to be a pretty close community of people based on how cohesive they are all working together. It seems that Kris and Nathan arrived just as they were getting ready to serve dinner. The smell of smoked meats fills the air.

There is an upper level like you see in most larger barns. There is a corner in the back that looks like a kitchen area. Several people are preparing food and operating like any busy kitchen. There is the immediate area where there are chairs set up, in rows, like a church. The inside is actually quite nice. The floors are clean with large area rugs throughout. There is even a small bar that is stocked with plenty of liquor. To the left, there are some old guitars and hubcaps hanging on the wall around a pool table in the corner, and also a small arsenal of guns. Moving further into the barn, there are farming tools hanging on the wall as well, a real one-stop-shop for your right to maintain and defend your land.

To the upper level from the center of the barn, there is a shiny brass cross mounted on the railing that hangs over the main hall. Kris and Nathan look at this cross, and as they look around, they are a little overstimulated, surprised, and confused. Jasper stops, turns around and gestures, "Phone's over there."

"Thanks," Nathan says. As Nathan and Kris walk over to the nicotine-white, 1980's landline telephone with the curly cord that hangs on the wall, someone knocks into Nathan, jarring him. Nathan turns to see who bumped him and it is Cliff, from earlier at the gas station. Cliff turns around and stares him down.

"Got something you wanna say to me?" Cliff hisses.

Kris puts his arm in front of Nathan, "Come on man. Let's just use the phone and get out of here," Kris warns. Nathan's face turns red and he is fuming all over again.

Cliff turns to walk away, with a smile on his face, feeling accomplished. "Yeeeeaaaah that's what I thought."

Nathan visibly takes a deep breath and bites his tongue. It physically pains him to not react.

Kris turns back to Cliff as he is walking away. 'Hey bro, seriously. What's your problem?"

Cliff turns to Kris, clearly waiting for a reaction from someone. "What's my problem?" Cliff takes a few steps toward Kris and Nathan. "I'll tell you what my problem is. Little sacks of shit like you and your friend here. You think you can come into our town, drivin' your fancy cars that park themselves, usin' your GPS, and disrespect me and my family." Cliff is beginning to raise his voice a bit now. "You got your smart phones but look like real dumb fucks without them, and you got the fuckin' nerve to look down on us!"

Kris looks at Nathan a little shocked. "Look man, I don't know about all that stuff you're saying, but we were just foolin' around earlier. You know, boys will be boys. That sorta thing," Kris explains.

Nathan turns to grab the phone and begins dialing, while Kris is talking to Cliff. Most of the folks in the barn are watching this situation as it unfolds, waiting for something to happen. Cliff gets face to face with Kris, and it's like he is feeding off the attention he is drawing. "You don't look like no boys. Pretty sure I seen't yous buying a couple of cases of beer earlier."

Kris is slow to respond now, treading each word carefully. Nathan nudges Kris and leans into his ear, "Yo, this phone isn't working."

Cliff looks at Kris and then at Nathan, grinning wide before it becomes laughter. Kris grabs the phone and hears no dial tone. "What the f–"

From the upper level a deep voice bellows loud. "Alright. That's enough." Everyone in the barn turns to the voice and it is Ozzy who steps forward, with his hands on the railing looking down, right above where the brass cross is hanging. Some people are watching him with looks of adoration. "Cliff, that's quite enough. Thank you."

Cliff smiles, backing off like an obedient guard dog, feeling accomplished as he is solely focused on Ozzy now.

Kris and Nathan look around, still holding the phone even more confused. Ozzy begins to walk down the stairs that run along the wall, his boots slamming into the wood heavily with each step. "Everyone. Let's give a hand for our guests this evening," he orders as he walks down the steps,

On command, everyone turns to Kris and Nathan and claps fanatically.

Kris scans the room, bewildered as to what is happening. So bizarre. Nathan does the same.

"What is this?" Nathan demands.

"Shhh! Ozzy's speaking. Show a little respect," one woman says from the gathering.

Kris hangs up the phone, and leans close to Nathan, "Dude, I think we need to get the fuck out of here *right now*," he whispers.

Kris and Nathan begin to walk toward the barn doors when Jasper and a few other guys grab them. "Have a seat, fellas. Stay a while," Jasper says, as he pushes Kris into a chair. Nathan is pushed into a seat as well by another guy.

"We're just gonna go," Kris says. Kris and Nathan try to get up and they are quickly pushed back down even more aggressively.

"What the fuck bro? I said we're going!" Nathan challenges.

"Well we are delighted to have you as our guests this evening," Ozzy chirps as he approaches. The crowd moves out of his way, like watching oil in water as he walks toward Kris and Nathan. Ozzy stands in front of them, as they sit confused, looking at Ozzy. Ozzy takes a moment, staring with his arms crossed.

"What are you doing?" Nathan asks.

"Well, you see that's just it son, I don't know just yet what I am doing… Nor what I'm going to do… But we will get there, in time," Ozzy enthused, with a playful and charismatic charm as he speaks.

"Look, sir, we just want to go. We don't want any trouble," Kris pleads.

Cliff replies from the crowd quickly, "Well it sure as shit looked like you wanted trouble earlier to–" Ozzy holds two fingers up and Cliff immediately falls silent.

Ozzy begins to pace slowly. Everyone in the room follows Ozzy's every move with their eyes and hangs onto his every movement, hungry for the next words to come out of his mouth. He has a certain charisma like that of a beloved stand-up comedian on stage, or an attorney who knows just the right way to connect with and finesse a jury. Ozzy speaks with the cadence of a southern preacher that is saturated with the coolness of a cowboy.

"Tonight we welcome our *young* guests. We welcome their energy, their passion, their youth, and their tenacity," Ozzy says with conviction, projecting for everyone in the barn to hear.

"We're not staying, man. Did you not hear us?" Nathan yells, in a nervous outburst, wearing a scowl on his face. He tries to stand again and two men restrain him. "Get the fuck off of me!" Nathan demands, kicking and is trying to get free. As he rises to his feet, one of the men holding him kicks the back of his leg and Nathan drops to his knees. The man who kicked him drops quickly to put him in a loose chokehold, with his knee against his back while the other guy has one of his wrists, and another woman rushes over to grab his other arm to hold him still.

Ozzy, without missing a beat, continues pacing the room. "You see, it's this sort of fight that got our attention in the first place. You think we wanted to fight? We didn't wanna fight. We are simple, peaceful, brothers, sisters, children of the light. You simply cast the first stone. And it's this fighting, angst, and resistance that the church shuns."

Kris watches Nathan fight and he looks at Jasper who is watching him, as Cliff is eyeing Nathan, just waiting for him to make a move or say something stupid. "We really didn't mean any disrespect," Kris stutters, "We were just messing around earlier, and things got carried away. It was really stupid and we see that. I'm sorry. Nate here is sorry. Nate, tell the man you're–"

Kris is interrupted by Jasper kicking a chair across the floor abruptly, and getting in Kris' face. "That's right boy! That was stupid! But you'd be wise to keep your mouth shut while Brother Ozzy speaks! …Brother Ozzy, please, continue." Jasper growled. Ozzy smiles like a proud father and gives a wink to Jasper.

"Kris… It's Kris right?" Kris breathes heavily with wide eyes staring at Ozzy. "You seem like a good kid. Bright future. All of the world at your feet." Ozzy walks over to Kris, and brushes off Kris' shoulders, "But you think you can just step on the world don'tcha?" Ozzy leans in close, and puts his index finger in the center of Kris' forehead. "You lack respect," Ozzy huffs. Ozzy stands and looks at the woman who was at the gas station earlier with them from across the barn. He extends his hand out. "Patty, dear, hand me my walkie please." Patty quickly fetches a walkie talkie from nearby and hustles it to him. "Thank you, dear," Ozzy says to Patty. Ozzy presses the talk button. "Homebase to Wild Turkey, got a copy? Over."

7

◇

Ozzy holds the walkie talkie, waiting for a response while staring around the room.

"Homebase, this is Wild Turkey. Pullin' up now. I got two rabbits and a whole lotta horsepower, over."

Ozzy smiles. "Well alrighty then Wild Turkey, bring 'em on in and let's get started. Over," he says through laughter. From outside a horn is honked, and you can hear the engine rattling in the frame of the vehicle outside of the barn doors. "Ladies and gentlemen, the rest of the party has arrived," Ozzy announces, wearing the smile of a politician. People begin to clap throughout the room as things are starting to feel more ceremonious. Two men open the doors and the bright headlights shine inside of the barn from the truck. He turns off the engine, leaves the lights on, and the driver side door swings open. Virgil steps out of the truck slowly, accompanied by a groan. Nathan, still restrained, looks on with growing fear as he notices Kris' Dodge hooked up to the back.

Kris notices and jumps to his feet "Why do you have my car!? Where's Mike and Liv!?" Cliff comes over and hits Kris across the face with a stiff forearm.

Virgil looks at Kris and Nathan. "Oh, so this must be one of your friends then." Virgil goes around to the bed of the truck and drags Mike out of the truck bed. The truck lights are blinding as Kris looks in that direction, squinting. Virgil is talking to Mike, as he is waking up and unsteady. "Come on now fella. Don't crash yet. Come on, come say hi to your friends, they've been waitin' to see you."

Kris tries to stand with his nose bloodied, looking toward the truck when he sees Mike's silhouette being shoved into the barn through the shining lights before he becomes visible. "MIKE!" Kris shouts. Mike falls onto his frontside, face-planting, still tied up at the wrists. He tries to stand and get to his feet.

Nathan looks on in full panic, still in the chokehold and being restrained. He sees Mike and shouts, "Fuck you, motherfuckers!"

People in the barn begin to laugh at Nathan's outburst. "Look, we've learned our lesson. What do you want from us? I apologized already! Do you want money?" Kris cries out to anyone that will listen.

Virgil walks in front of the truck lights, casting a moving shadow across the barn. He walks to the passenger side door. "Money?" Virgil asks, followed by a playful chuckle. "Naw, we don't want ya money, no no." He opens the door and Olivia falls out. Virgil catches her and drags her out carefully. "We just want common decency like anyone else." After Virgil drags Olivia into the barn, he leaves her on the ground, still wrapped in chains and twine.

Nathan sees her and he becomes enraged. He tries to stand and his sudden burst of energy catches the guys holding him off guard. "NOOOO!" Nathan screams. He throws the guy applying the chokehold off of him like he is in an MMA fight. "You leave her alone!" Nathan pushes one guy who tries to get a better grip of him. With his newly freed hand, he punches the other guy across the face as hard as he can. Nathan stumbles hard as he puts all of his weight into the punch, and as he turns around after catching his balance, Jasper is there with a fist full of rings on a collision course, right into Nathan's right eye, sending him crashing to the ground. Olivia looks on at her boyfriend, with her mouth gagged still, as he is clobbered by Jasper's mean, ring-ladened left jab.

Olivia looks on helplessly, with tears streaming down her face. Mike struggles to stand as he looks on, unable to do anything. Kris stands there and guys surround him expecting him to make a move at any moment. Tension is at its peak as they look on with panic setting in, this is fight or flight. Hearts beating like a bouncing bass note. Nathan grimaces and rolls onto his back while holding his eye, letting out a sigh of pain. "Aaaaaaaaaah," he exhales. "Fuck!" Jasper stands over him in a defensive position, a position of power. Nathan rolls to his side and tries to stand.

Jasper takes a couple steps back and he begins to clap. "Well alright then. Looks like we got ourselves a warrior here." Jasper crouches slowly, admiring Nathan. "Kid, I just knocked the piss out of you and you got right back up. I gotta say. I'm impressed."

Cliff shouts out, "Looks like our premier athlete can take a hit after all."

Jasper and Cliff walk over to Nathan and grab his arms at both sides and take him over near Mike and Olivia. Two other men grab Kris by the arms and usher him over as well. The three all stare at one another, scared, wanting nothing more than for this to be some cruel prank that they do in the rural parts of the country. Nathan's eye swells quickly. Nathan is on his knees while Kris, Mike, and Olivia stand there. A man walks up and cuts Mike's twine loose, freeing his hands, and removing his gag. Virgil goes to Olivia and removes the gag from her mouth and takes the chains off of her as well. Virgil takes the chains and walks over to his truck and tosses them into the bed of the truck and begins to lower the car. Once the car is lowered, he makes quick work of detaching it and leaving it where it is.

Ozzy looks the four in their eyes and gives a slight nod. "Alright. Gang's all here… Welcome to the party." He hops up onto a table in the common area of the barn. "Brothers and sisters," he projects. "Tonight the righteous shall exile those who look down on us!"

In a united mess of voices, the crowd, which is more of a small mob, is responding to Ozzy's words with a mix of praises and cheers.

"Earlier today, these young people chose to pick on us. Simply because they seen't a van full of simple, older folks… Now that ain't right, is it?"

The crowd reactions ensue as Ozzy speaks directly to his community. The people are eating out of his hand and he knows it. "Is it because they think we're weak? …We maintain an easy life out here …We rely on the land as much as we can. We work together, eat, drink, even pray together… And these ungrateful, self-centered," Ozzy turns to Nathan and his facial expression melts into a look of disgust, *"heathens*… from out there, they represent everything about a generation. A generation that comes from a world that done forgot about us!"

The crowd becomes louder and more riotous with every statement.

"That think they can walk all over us," he continues to preach.

Kris looks around the barn and notices, right by the front doors, his spare tire leaning against the wall. He notices it because it looks brand new and has the dodge logo on the wheel. Kris looks at Ozzy from his knees, "You guys planned this!" Kris accuses. "You guys planned all of this! The car, everything!" Kris stands and takes a few steps toward Ozzy before Cliff and Jasper step in his way. "What are you guys going to do? Are you going to kill us?" he asks, looking right at Jasper.

Ozzy continues his sermon, without acknowledging Kris at all. "They come into our town. Talking down to us. Looking down on us! Their entitlement must be punished."

The crowd inside is very worked up now making lots of noise.

"They've become too dependent on technology and gotten too far away from one another. The connection has created a huge disconnect!"

The crowd cheers angrily and some fists are raised into the air.

"They're not like us, brothers and sisters! We got each other!" Ozzy says with deep conviction.

The crowd shouts again, "Yeah!"

"We've always had each other. That's all we've ever needed."

The crowd cheers once more.

"They don't have their smartphones." Ozzy jumps down off of the table. "They don't have their GPS." Ozzy walks between his people as he looks at Kris. "They ain't got no car." Ozzy walks between Jasper and Cliff and right over to Kris, getting in Kris' face. Ozzy smirks and snickers to himself, brushing off Kris' shoulders and the front of his shirt. "And they ain't got no chance in hell."

The crowd offers a mix of applause and cheers to Ozzy, who pauses until the cheering subsides.

"While they still have each other, they don't have the things they value as essential. But we still have each other." Ozzy walks over and is standing in front of Mike, Olivia, Nathan and Kris.

Cliff grabs Kris by his arm and pushes him to turn around and face his friends now. He digs the front of his foot into the back of Kris' leg making him fall to his knees again.

"You're gonna wanna stay down for this part," Cliff whispers.

Ozzy paces slowly with one arm crossed, gripping his elbow, and his other hand stroking his chin.

"What are you going to do with us?" Olivia asks, anxiously watching him pace.

Ozzy walks over to Olivia and squats down, getting eye level with her. "Awww, darlin', don't you worry. We're gonna let you walk right out of here in just a moment." Mike, Nathan and Kris look up after hearing that and they aren't sure what to expect. Ozzy stands and calls out to Patty. "Patty, my dear?"

Patty steps out from the crowd answering his summon quickly. She goes to his side, "Yes, love?" Patty replies.

Ozzy looks up, and takes a breath. "Would you be so kind as to bring me my ax?"

Patty looks at Ozzy, and then darts a sharp glance at Olivia. "Yes, my love." Patty walks away, and Ozzy begins pacing again.

"You know, I was young like y'all once. Everyone in this room was. We never acted out like you did today though. Respect is currency and you are piss poor from what I can tell. So here's how this is gonna go,"

Patty comes through and hands Ozzy a wood ax that looks like it's seen its fair share of use. The handle is wrapped and worn looking. The head of the ax looks heavy, as one would normally look, but the edge shined as if it were just sharpened. The light from the truck shining inside hits the blade of the ax like a clean sterling silver, shimmering like clean jewelry. "Thank you, sweetheart," Ozzy says to Patty as he leans in and kisses her.

Ozzy admires the ax. "So today, you are going to learn two things. Number one, respect is earned, and respect should be paid. You have no respect, so something else will have to do." Ozzy looks at each of them for a moment, studying them each carefully when he fixates on Nathan, and he walks with a purpose over to him, raises the ax and swings it around to his back. Ozzy positions his feet to compensate for the weight and then pulls it from behind his back and over his head, slamming it down, crashing into Nathan's head with a punishing blow.

8

◇

"NOOOO!" Olivia cries out instantly as tears stream down her face.

"No! Nate!" Mike screams, stricken with panic.

Kris is frozen, shocked, offering no reaction as absolute horror overcomes him.

Ozzy tries to remove the ax from Nathan's head and it is stuck. He puts his boot on Nathan's face to get enough leverage to pull the ax out of his head, pulling as hard as he can and there is audible crunch from the bone separating and cracking as he pulls. The ax comes free and it flings a stream of blood out. Ozzy stumbles a little and turns to the remaining three with blood spatter on his face now. "And number two… Wrong bus motherfuckers!"

Olivia looks on and everything around her goes quiet, like muffled chaos around her. Everything is blurry, out of focus, and in slow motion. She sees faces around the room but can't distinguish the expressions. She just watched her boyfriend be executed and the situation is beginning to feel more hopeless by the second. Kris, from his knees, falls forward and catches himself with his hands. His eyes are screaming where his voice fails him. The shock of him watching his childhood best friend be murdered weighs heavy. Mike watches on, paralyzed by fear. Nathan was a close and longtime friend of Mike's. What should have been a fun weekend back home with friends and family, has turned into a detour into hell.

"Alright. You guys, go ahead and clean this shit up," Ozzy orders. Cliff and Jasper go over to Nathan's body and lift him up into a wheelbarrow. Nathan's large frame hangs out of the small wheelbarrow very awkwardly. Olivia is fixated on the pool of blood on the ground.

Kris looks up at Ozzy with a genuine look of hatred plastered to his face. "You motherfucker! I dare you to try that shit, just me and you! Come on!" Kris howls. Ozzy just stares at Kris as he comes unglued. "Come on bitch! Bring it! You fuckin' pussy! I can see you ain't shit without all of your little –"

BAM! Ozzy cracks Kris in the nose with the handle of the ax. "Dammit boy, don't make me go and do something crazy now!" Ozzy looks at the ax and chuckles to himself. Kris' nose is bloodied instantly as he falls onto his back. Ozzy walks over to Patty and hands her the ax. 'Patty, my dear, would you be a doll and put this away?"

Patty looks into his eyes. "Yes, honey." Ozzy wipes his hands with a bit of showmanship as he turns back to his audience.

Ozzy looks over at Mike, who stares up at him with tears streaming down his face. "You look like hell, boy!" Ozzy chirps at Mike who looks away, like a submissive dog. Ozzy then turns to Kris. "Shit son, the way you talk to me, you'd think that kid was your best friend wouldn't you?" Ozzy smiles and a few people in the room laugh. Ozzy then looks over at Olivia, who is still frozen and shaken up. Ozzy crouches down to her level and looks her in the eyes. Her eyes meet his and she is crippled with a flood of emotions. "What's the matter sweetheart?" he asks, brushing the back of his hand against her cheek as she jerks away. He offers up a subtle laugh. He is quite amused at this entire situation right now, and this behavior says just how comfortable he is on the main stage. Ozzy puts his thumb on her chin and two fingers under it and turns her to face him again. "Awww I think I get it. That wasn't just your friend was it? Did I just… Was that… Was that your… *boyfriend*?" Olivia's face tense as Ozzy is now just taunting her. She is seething and taking fast breaths as they lock eyes. "Yeah, I've seen that look before. That pretty face, those eyes. Everything about you. You're lookin' at me like I'm the devil or somethin'." Olivia impulsively spits in his face as her rage has come to the surface now. Ozzy closes his eyes and stands up. He wipes the spit from his face with his bare hands, while laughing some more.

Cliff and Jasper return to the circle and look over Kris, Mike, and Olivia. Jasper stands beside Mike and taps him playfully on his shoulder. "Just think, if your buddy would have just not pulled our chain, maybe the left and right side of his head might still be together," Jasper says with a smirk.

Cliff laughs out loud and some of the others in the barn offer up laughter as well. "Yeah, he was actin' all kinds of tough earlier," Cliff hollers. "And now he looks like–" Cliff makes a face that is supposed to be of a dead person with their eyes rolled back. Cliff laughs even harder, and others join in.

Kris is holding his nose as blood runs through his hands, down his forearms, and the front of his shirt. He stands once more, looking at Jasper with fire in his eyes. He lets go of his nose and holds his head up with a raging confidence. "I'm going to kill you," he growls through the curdling blood that is draining down his throat.

Jasper's laughing turns serious as people continue to enjoy themselves around him when he walks over to Kris, pointing to his own chest and looking around. "Who? ...me? ...You're going to kill ...me?" Kris stares at Jasper breathing heavily with primitive, instinctual rage over his blood covered face. Mike and Olivia look on anxiously. Jasper stands face to face with Kris, hoping someone tries to make a move.

Ozzy interrupts the tension. "Alright. The time has come."

All eyes are on Ozzy now and Patty stands at his side like a loyal servant. Cliff and Jasper go to his other side like trained hyenas. Mike, Kris, and Olivia look on, waiting for what comes next in what feels like a sick game where Ozzy and his merry band of *saints* are the cat, and they are the mouse. Ozzy steps up onto a wooden picnic table that is near the center of the floor. With the brass cross at his back, he looks down on everyone. "Tonight, the ceremony begins again. It has been nearly two hundred days since we last offered praise to our Lord. Another season is upon us as the summer brings warmth to our land, and life to our fields, and we prepare to harvest our crops. We pray for health, and pray for our community under your wisdom and loving light." The crowd watches Ozzy as if he holds the cure to the plague. Confidence oozes from him as he radiates positive energy with each word spoken. Everyone is eager and ready to give praise. "Brothers… Sisters… Please join me in this festival of life, as we celebrate our God, and we become His arms. We will bring down His divine hand of swift justice onto the fiends of this world." Everyone becomes rowdy in response to Ozzy's sermon. Fists are raised in excitement as Ozzy speaks passionately. Cheers help to carry Ozzy's passion as he has absolute power over his people.

Mike stands up, and Olivia as well. Olivia begins to look around. The three know that nothing good is going to come of this. Kris stands, poised to fight, while Mike remains uneasy. Olivia looks to the barn doors and sees the truck there still, and the doors open. Virgil and two other men block the large doorway. She looks at the walls around her and sees the wall of weapons and tools, but they are too far from where she is at to be able to get to without someone stopping her. Panic begins to weigh down on her as this situation becomes more hopeless by the second.

Ozzy looks down to Patty. "It's time."

Patty walks over to where Nathan's body was. Where the blood from his head is still pooled on the ground, Patty kneels down and dips her finger tips in the blood. She stands, looking at Ozzy as she places the bloodied fingertips high on her cheekbones, with two fingers, one on each side of her nose, and she draws lines down to her chin, leaving what looks like a bloody skull or some sort of war paint on her face. She fires a sharp glance at Kris, and then at Olivia for a moment, before she turns to the brass cross and closes her eyes.

Ozzy hops down from the table and walks over to Mike. "Here's what we're going to do now." Ozzy places his hands on Mike's shoulders, then brushes off the dirt from his shoulders and chest. "You're going to get to walk out of here tonight." He goes over to Kris, looks at his nose, "Oooo that is definitely broken." He continues walking toward Olivia now while he is talking. "That's right. We will let you go. Leave. No catch. You just have to escape." Olivia, and Mike lock eyes, confused. "I get it. You're wondering, 'Why?' Why now?' …Well, we here at the church like to play this little game every now and again where we get us some young bloods, much like yourselves here, and basically play hide and seek, which usually turns into tag, but with a crossbow or buck knife. Usually something wicked-sharp."

Mike takes a couple steps forward. "What if we don't wanna play your game?"

Ozzy looks at Mike, stunned, "That's a fair question, young man. But it's simple really. If you choose to not play, it will not be as fun for us, but also not as much fun for you either. You like to have fun don't ya? Or are you some kind of sissy boy who hates fun?" Mike stares back offering no reaction. "If you can survive until the sun comes up, you get to live. Simple as that. If you happen to live, and go tellin' the cops though, well, things might not end up so well for the cops. And who's to say we don't go find you? Maybe ya family. Maybe we are the police in this town, you don't know… Of course, no one has actually escaped yet. We're miles from anything and all the neighbors nearby, well… Most of them are here watching."

Hearts are beating heavier now amongst the three. A sense of dread looms in the air, as there are so many smiling faces throughout the room chomping at the bit to begin.

"Is everyone ready?" Ozzy surveys, arms spread wide as a flurry of positive affirmations rain down on him. He looks at a woman off to the side and gives her a nod and she pulls a sheet off of a rolling cart. She pushes the cart to Ozzy and has several masks fashioned to resemble predatory animals. They appear to be homemade with paper mache, most of them white. The woman begins pushing the cart and handing out masks to those who wish to partake in the festivities. "We are the elders of this land, the apex predators so we hunt on this land just like God intended." The rowdy group is fully engaged with what Ozzy has to say. The woman continues handing out these masks and folks are slipping them on.

"So my brothers here are gonna step aside and you three are free to leave. Run away in any direction as fast as you'd like. Hide should you choose to… We'll give you a 60 second head start even. How's that sound?" Ozzy asks, with a playful smirk and a wink. The three look at him with no response at all. Jasper puts on a dirty white bear mask that is a little silly looking under normal circumstances. Cliff takes a wolf mask from the woman and jabs Jasper as the two walk over to the wall with all of the weapons and tools. Several people from the crowd join them.

Ozzy holds a hand straight up in the air, "Aaaaaand GO!" he shouts as he swings his arm down like a referee at a race track. Olivia and Mike turn to leave and look behind them to see if anyone is going to stop them. No one follows at all. Several folks wearing the unsettling masks watch them. Kris follows them immediately out through the open barn doors. With the barn at their backs, the three of them scatter out into the lot with no plan at all, only escaping and trying to survive.

Patty's voice rings out from the barn as they're running.

"One   Mississippi…   Two   Mississippi…   Three Mississippi…"

9

◇

Olivia is on the move, like a rabbit being chased by a hungry dog, in this case, several dogs. Eyes looking ahead, head straight, focused on getting far away, and quickly. Kris is alongside her, but much faster and also much more frantic. He slows down and is looking around. He looks at cars and everything that is in the area of the dirt lot. Mike is not far behind but he seems like he might be concussed because he is moving slower than the others. Olivia darts past all of the cars between the barn and the gas station. She passes the gas station and reaches the road. She stands in the middle of the road and looks in both directions "HELLOOOO! …HEEEELP!" she screams.

Patty's counting can still be heard from the road as Olivia looks around, trying to decide her next move.

"Eight Mississippi… Nine Mississippi…" is heard in the distance.

Mike is in front of the gas station, banging on the glass door. He kicks the door trying to break the glass but it's just too thick to be broken that easily. He looks around and finds a cinder block. He picks up the cinder block and carries it over to the window.

"Twenty five…. Twenty six…" -

Mike lifts the cinder block up over his head and with two hands and a grunt he throws it into the door as hard as he can and the glass shatters into a million tiny pieces, making a ton of noise in the process. A flashing light inside goes off and a loud constant ringing sings like a beacon, a loud ringing that basically screams *'HEY! OVER HERE!'* Mike steps through the door carefully.

Kris is looking around the cars in the lot. He is looking inside windows and checking doors. He finds an SUV with the door unlocked and opens it. He is looking around the floors and under the seats. He continues checking vehicles as he finds nothing of use.

He checks an older beat up sedan with the hood ripped completely off. Nothing but sun-beaten and cracked leather seats inside, and the smell of cigarette ashes and dusty, moldy fabric hit his nostrils. He leaves the door open and goes to the next. It's a pickup truck with the windshield missing and both the driver side and passenger side doors removed. He leans inside and sees some clothes and an ashtray overflowing with cigarette butts. He goes to the bed of the truck where he sees some trash scattered and a crow bar with chipped yellow paint on it. He grabs the crow bar and starts looking around for Mike and Olivia.

"…Forty! …Forty one!"

Olivia is in the middle of the road looking around, wondering what to do now. Her scream is answered only by the sounds of her own voice bouncing back. She turns back to the barn and sees no one coming out, but Patty can still be heard counting. She sees Mike break the glass to the gas station and the alarm ringing gets her attention. As she sees Mike walk into the gas station, she walks toward the broken glass. Kris approaches from the lot with the crowbar in hand. "Olivia!" Kris calls out. He waves her over.

" ...Forty nine ...Fifty!" -

Olivia goes over to Kris as he leans in close, "You need to find something sharp or like… something hard you can fight with," Kris urges her, trying to speak over the alarm.

"Fuck! Fuck! Fuck! Running out of time. I should run! Should I run? What's Mike doing?" Olivia asks, frantically.

"No! Don't run. We need to hide and see who comes out." Kris pleads.

"Why are we waiting to see who comes out?" Olivia asks.

Kris holds up the crowbar, "So I can bash someone's head in with this thing. Let's go. We need to hide and wait." Kris grabs Olivia's hand and heads over to the row of cars in the lot. They crouch down and walk between a smashed up van with the wood paneling on the side and a wrecked car. Kris slides the door open on the van. Olivia drops to the ground, in the dirt, and scurries underneath the car right next to it. Patches of wild grass and weeds growing throughout the lot offer Olivia limited visibility, but just enough.

Meanwhile, in the gas station...

Mike walks inside and past the potato chips, past the snack cakes and candy bars, and is looking around the automotive part of the store where there are some basic tools and sort of cheap, random items. Mike sees pliers, screwdrivers, hammers. He grabs a basic claw hammer from the hook. He then looks around the counter and sees an acrylic display on the counter that has weed bowls and fancy looking pocket knives. He sets the hammer down and grabs a folding knife that has jagged teeth on the backside of the blade, and has a super colorful and abstract paint design on the handle. The blade is about four inches and matte black. He puts the knife into his pocket.

He goes behind the counter and looks around, and underneath the counter there is a sawed-off shotgun mounted on two hooks. He grabs the shotgun, opens it to see that it's already loaded. He rummages around a small cabinet underneath the counter and finds a mess of random things in each of the drawers. Among the mess, he finds a box of shotgun shells. He takes two and puts them into the gun and then quickly grabs a handful and puts them into his pocket. With the alarm screaming still, and a shotgun in hand, he creeps over to the door and peeks out, looking to see if anyone is coming, or if he can see Kris or Olivia anywhere.

"Fifty eight... Fifty nine... Fifty nine and a half..."

Patty takes a deep breath and sighs.

"Sixty!"

10

The Hunt

Patty reaches sixty, and as she has been counting, several people have been preparing weapons for the hunt and putting the masks on that look like nothing short of a children's art project.

Jasper grabs a hatchet from the wall and begins sharpening it with a flintstone. Sparks shoot away from him as he grinds it along the blade with a continuous rhythm. Another kind of chubby man grabs a softball bat that looks like it is relatively new. He is cleaning it with the bottom of his shirt. "Hey Jimbo, you ever think bout' trying one of them wooden ones? They're a little heavier," Cliff asks while adjusting the tension cord on a crossbow.

"Naw, I kind of like the 'dink' sound this one makes," Jimbo grins.

Virgil and another man draped in a filthy flannel and ripped up jeans, stand at the wall, admiring the selection as they try to decide what they will use for the hunt. "I think I might go with the machete this time around, whuddaya think, hmm?" the man in greasy clothes asks. Virgil looks at this man curiously. "Hmph. Well Greaseball, I reckon you could use the machete, or maybe a pickaxe."

Greaseball holds the machete and pantomimes what it might be like to slice through the air like a samurai. He looks over at the pickaxe that hangs on the wall with a look of disapproval, and then back at the machete. "I think the machete will do just fine," Greaseball assures himself while trying to get amped up, bouncing around and talking to himself. "Imma get 'em. I already got 'em! Please, oh please Lord. Let me catch one of 'em and be the one who does the smitin' for You, in Your name, oh Lord." Greaseball exudes imagination and high energy as he takes his place in line, standing beside a much larger man. "You ready Buck? This gon' be a fun one."

Buck is a little more relaxed in comparison. He is a tall, beefy guy with a bald head, scruffy beard, like you might see on a viking. "I've been waiting for another go at this for months," Buck says with plenty of bravado in his voice as he swings a sledgehammer in slow motion like it's a golf club, waiting to begin.

Patty calmly walks over to the wall and grabs a large knife from a shelf. She undoes the snap button and slides it carefully out of the leather sheath and holds it up, admiring the blade for a moment. Satisfied with her choice, she turns to Ozzy who is on one knee, much like a royal knight, facing the brass cross that hangs overhead. He is praying and mouthing words to himself with his eyes closed and head bowed.

Ozzy rises to his feet, completely invigorated as everyone waits for him. He walks over to Patty, stands in front of her, looking into her eyes as he places his hands on her shoulders and smiles proudly. "I am so lucky you found me honey." Ozzy pulls her into his embrace and gives her a warm and sensual hug.

She looks up to him and they kiss. "I love you Oz. You've added so much to my life," Patty responds gratefully.

"I love you too," and he kisses her again. "It's time to do God's work dear." Patty nods, and as they separate she joins the other guys who are waiting to go hunting.

Ozzy begins to pace the floor behind them. With his hands behind his back, and his boots landing heavy with each step. "Tonight, we cleanse the earth of the unjust… the unruly…"

Everyone listens closely with an abundance of adoration and respect for their leader. It's almost as if God were saying these words Himself.

"We contest with the bacteria that continues to fester into the society we've lived in, and protected for much of our lives," Ozzy says, with erratic movements. His cadence and delivery is like a baptist preacher who loves a little showmanship with his words. He is getting more into his zone as he speaks, changing the pitch of his voice to really captivate the audience.

"Yeah!" the crowd cheers in unison.

"This is our corner of the world."

"Yeah!" the crowd cheers once more, with a mix of affirmations to be heard.

"Nobody is gonna cast judgment on any of our brothers or sisters!"

The small mob begins to move around a little more and their cheers take on a little more life, responding to Ozzy's statements. The cheers match Ozzy's energy as they roar.

Ozzy walks over to the wall purposefully, grabbing a four pointed, rusted pitchfork off of the wall. He turns to face everyone. "Should you so choose to treat *MY* brothers and sisters like they're somehow lesser… well that's just what you gon' get from God… You will be judged as 'lesser'."

Cliff stands with his crossbow over his shoulder as the commotion continues. "Fuck yeah, brother! Motherfucking hounds of justice! Y'all ready to do this shit?" Cliff begins to howl like a wolf as others join in.

Ozzy raises his hand up and immediately everyone falls silent, watching him, waiting for his command. As the silence in the barn ensues, the alarm still rings from the front of the lot at the convenience store. Ozzy scans the room, looking at his brothers and sisters, with pride gleaming from his face. He closes his raised hand into a solid fist. Those participating in this hunt immediately leave the barn. Those who aren't participating are older men and women, homemakers and helping hands who help keep things tidy and bellies full. The people who aren't really built for this type of activity,

"Well, let's get to work," Jasper says, twirling his hatchet.

Those taking part in the hunt step out. Patty and Jasper pace slowly and observe everything around them carefully. Greaseball, Jimbo, Virgil, and Buck walk out ahead looking like a ragtag redneck biker gang. Buck clutches his sledgehammer with two hands close to his chest. Jimbo has his bat resting on his shoulder. Greaseball is a ball of energy with erratic body language and a machete to keep things interesting.

Jimbo veers off to the right and is looking behind the gas station and looking around the dumpster behind it. "I'll check out the store."

Greaseball taps Buck to get his attention, pointing to their left toward the line of smashed vehicles. Jasper heads into the fields of tall grass and bushes that are behind this row of cars.

Patty follows him into the grass. Cliff continues to walk out to the road with his crossbow.

Buck and Greaseball walk along the cars on high alert for any movement or signs of where their targets may have gone. Greaseball walks between vehicles, looking into the windows closely, scraping the tip of the machete on the glass. Buck paces along the front ends of the cars cautiously looking around. "Here boy!" Greaseball calls out as he whistles like he is calling for a dog. "Where are ya?" Greaseball starts opening car doors. As he does this, he is getting closer to the van that Kris is hiding in. Kris hears all of this going on and can hear Greaseball getting closer as car doors open and slam. He sits off to the side of the door gripping the crowbar tight, waiting for someone to slide the door open.

Olivia is under the car next to the van, just across from the sliding door. She lies there watching Buck's feet pass by with her hands over her mouth, desperate to cage any audible fear. She hears Greaseball whistling and can feel him getting closer with each car door slammed. The ringing is still sounding off at the gas station.

Jimbo is poking around behind the gas station convenience store. He looks behind the dumpster, lifting the heavy plastic door to look inside. He flips it all the way open and uses his bat to move trash around. He sees nothing of interest and closes the lid. He then walks around the front and sees the light from inside flashing. As he gets to the front door he sees where the glass door has been shattered and the cinder block is inside the doorway. Jimbo peeks his head in and prepares himself in a defensive position as he takes a few careful steps inside, looking around.

The convenience store is dark and the flashing lights from the alarm aren't making it any easier to see if someone is in there or hear if anyone is making any noise. Jimbo goes over to the circuit box and opens the door to it and sees all of the switches. Jimbo hits the switches and the ringing falls silent as the flashing lights die.

Mike is behind the counter, crouched down hiding, waiting, as the alarm is silenced and the lights stop flashing. With a sawed-off shotgun in hand, he tries to steady his breathing as he listens to Jimbo moving throughout the store. The sound of glass shards wedged into the boot treads with each step can be heard clearly. Jimbo's heavy footsteps sink into the wooden floor like a lion's roar with each slow step. Jimbo stops and looks around as his eyes adjust to the darkness. Only the moonlight from outside, and the dimly-lit, flickering readerboard near the road illuminates anything inside. "I know you're in here… Why don't you come on out now?"

Jimbo waits for some sort of noise or movement as Mike sits perfectly still underneath the counter on the floor, clutching the shotgun. Jimbo takes slow steps over to the coolers. He opens up one of the coolers and grabs a tall can of beer from the top display. "Hm, help yourself… Thanks… Don't mind if I do," Jimbo says to himself with a chuckle, as he opens the can and takes a big drink right there in front of the cooler. He walks around with a can of beer in one hand, and the softball bat in the other. "Come on now… Come have a drink with me, don't make me drink alone… Let's get to know each other."

Jimbo walks into the back area where the bathroom is and pushes open the bathroom door with the head of the bat and leans his head in to find nothing. Just a filthy bathroom. "Yooooo hooooo," he taunts playfully as he takes another sip from the tall can. He lets the door shut and heads over toward the counter. He sees the wall of cigarettes and has his eyes fixed on them. With another sip he sets the can on the counter and wipes his mouth off and walks around the counter to look closer at the tobacco selection, with his softball bat wedged under his arm. As Jimbo grabs a pack of cigarettes and starts to mash the top of the pack against his palm before he opens them, Mike sits there watching Jimbo's legs, as still as can be, trying not to make a noise.

Jimbo opens the pack of cigarettes, pulls one out, and puts it between his lips. He turns around to the counter and picks up one of the cheap plastic lighters near the register. Jimbo knocks over the can of beer when he grabs the lighter. The can falls onto the floor right at Mike's feet. Jimbo reacts, annoyed. "Shit!" he mutters as he lays the bat on the counter and crouches down, scrambling to pick the can up. Jimbo's eyes meet Mike's with surprise as he notices the shotgun on Mike's lap. Mike panics and rushes to his feet, shoving Jimbo out of the way. Mike has the stock of the gun in his left hand and the barrel in the right and pushes Jimbo against the back wall, knocking a bunch of cigarette packs off of the display as they spill onto the floor.

"GOD DAMMIT, you little cocksucker, I'm gonna teach you-" Jimbo grabs Mike and pushes him into the counter and tries to snatch the gun away, attempting to keep the barrel pointed away from him rather than him trying to actually take it. Jimbo is trying to wrestle the gun away from Mike with no luck but Mike is cornered behind the counter with Jimbo blocking him in.

Jimbo pushes Mike back against the side counter and pressees the gun against Mike's chest with one arm. He reaches with his other hand behind him to his left to grab the bat that he placed on the counter. Mike sees him grab the bat and every move he makes is fast, no thinking, just reacting. His eyes go wide, like alarms while the expression on his face screams *panic*. Jimbo swings the bat one-handed as hard as he can just as fast as he grips it. Mike leans forward, ducking, and burying his head into Jimbo's body and pushing him as hard as he can.

"AAAARGH!" Mike yells as he pushes Jimbo into a wire rack with hats on it, knocking Jimbo flat on his back, dropping the bat. Mike keeps the gun, and regains his balance.

Jimbo rolls onto his side, looking for the bat. "You little motherfucker, when I get my hands on you, you're as dead as your little friend back there. All-a-you are dead!"

Mike's face is painted with rage and he kicks the bat out of Jimbo's reach, and then kicks him in the face. Mike stands over him, looking down at him and aims the shotgun at his face. "Please don't make me do this!" Mike yells. Jimbo tries to get up and Mike puts his foot on his chest and pushes him back to the floor. "Stay on the floor! I will blow your fucking face off. I don't want to do it, but I will!"

Jimbo pushes Mike's foot off of his chest and looks him in the face as he tries to get up again. "Do what you're gonna do then!" Jimbo hisses. Mike stares at him almost in shock, frozen. "Do it! Pull the trigger you pussy! Ain't you got balls?"

Mike has an impulse as Jimbo is yelling at him from the floor and Mike presses the barrel to Jimbo's chest, pushing him back onto the floor with authority. "ARGH!" Mike lets out a fury-laced yell with his finger squeezing the trigger.

11

◇

Meanwhile, outside in the car lot.

Moments after the alarms have stopped and the flashing lights have been turned off, Greaseball checks the smashed up sedan just next to the van that Kris is hiding in. Kris sits as still as stone, clutching the crowbar with both hands, ready to pounce the second that the door opens. Buck walks ahead still looking around. Olivia no longer can see his feet from the car she is hiding underneath. Olivia hears where Greaseball is walking around the van and then she sees his feet right next to her. She tries her hardest not to move. As she is lying on her stomach, as still as can be, she notices a long flathead screwdriver, like a mechanic might use in the dirt, just out of her reach.

Greaseball stands outside of the van, near the sliding door, as Olivia's face is within inches of his feet. Kris is wound up and ready inside. Greaseball grabs onto the door handle and just as he is about to open the door, a gunshot echoes through the lot from the convenience store.

BOOM!

Like thunder clapping and roaring through the night. Greaseball turns his head away from the van quickly to look in the direction of the convenience store. He sees Buck out by the road looking at him and Buck shrugs, confused and he begins walking toward the storefront. Greaseball turns to look into the van and before he can even see Kris, he is struck in the face with a precise swing, as Kris grips a crowbar.

Greaseball puts his arms over his head to protect himself. "Ow! Fucking Christ!" he cries. He is disoriented and swings the machete wildly. Kris manages to avoid being hit with the machete and finds the opening to slide over and kick Greaseball in his chest, knocking him out of the van. Greaseball's back smashes against the car next to the van, and he knocks the passenger side mirror off. Kris is quick, lunging out of the van, tackling Greaseball even harder than the kick. Kris delivers several close range strikes with the crowbar to Greaseball's arms and ribs. Greaseball takes another big, wild swing with the machete that misses. Kris counters, kicking his forearm against the door of the car causing Greaseball to drop the machete.

Olivia sees the machete fall to the ground, but Kris inadvertently kicks it away as she watches feet scuffling through the struggle. She sees the dancing feet kicking up dirt and feels the car shaking as she hides. The fighting and noise gets Buck's attention and he walks over, with his sledgehammer, ready to go. Kris has Greaseball off balance. He grabs him by the front of the shirt and drags him out into the open part of the lot and slings him, rolling him onto his back. "It's on now, you old fuck!" Kris snaps, climbing on top of him, punching him in the face with the crowbar still in his clenched fist. Greaseball lets out a laugh after Kris stops. Kris stares at him for a moment as Greaseball continues his laughter and Kris sends another fist crashing down into his mouth.

Greaseball laughs a little harder as Kris stands up and is standing over Greaseball, watching him laugh hysterically. "You have no clue, how ab-so-lutely FUCKED you really are!" Greaseball heaves through a bloody mouth and misplaced laughter. Unsettled by Greaseball's maniacal glee, Kris raises the crowbar high above his head, and with all of his weight, drives the straight end right through Greaseball's eye, quieting the laughter instantly. Blood begins pooling, spreading fast underneath his head. It would appear the crowbar went all the way through his eye and the back of his skull. Kris lets go of the crowbar and falls to the ground, backing aways from the body. With a crowbar through his head and pillow of his own blood under him, his lifeless body remains smiling. Kris is still very amped up and jumps to his feet when he sees Buck coming at him with a sledgehammer in hand, and a very clear intent. Kris goes for the crowbar, yanking it out of Greaseball's head.

"Come on bitch!" Kris taunts, from a defensive position with the freshly seasoned, bloody crowbar, ready to fight.

Buck approaches and looks down at Greaseball, "Semper Fi brother." Buck turns his attention to Kris and he swings the hammer around to his back and raises the sledgehammer, and slams it down at Kris with a huff. Kris falls backwards to avoid what would have for sure been a fatal blow. The ground shakes around them from the slam of the hammerhead. The impact leaves an indent in the ground as Buck continues his assault. Kris scoots back quickly as the lumbering giant looks down at him, towering over him, making slow strides as he looks at Kris.

Buck rotates his shoulders back to prepare another big blow. Kris quickly backs away when he sees Olivia run out and jump on Buck's back. Buck drops the hammer while he spins around and tries reaching back to grab her. She screams like an animal, hanging on like a rodeo bull. She has the flathead screwdriver from under the car, and she starts to stab him in the shoulders and his back with it. Kris scrambles to his feet and goes over and hits Buck in the knee with the crowbar causing him to stagger and fall to one knee. Kris takes a swing at Buck's head and he reaches up and grabs the crowbar. He looks Kris in the eyes as he easily overpowers him and twists the crowbar, forcing his wrist to move in a way it's not supposed to, and Kris releases it quickly. Buck tosses the crowbar across the lot like a toothpick.

"ARGHHH!" Buck cries out, with Olivia still on his back, stabbing him ferociously.

She screams, stabbing and stabbing with rapid succession. "AHH! AHH! AHH!" she screams with each stab. Kris lays on the ground, his scared eyes meeting the big man's when Olivia jams the screwdriver into his left ear. Kris maintains eye contact as he watches the lights go out in Buck's eyes. He falls over, and Olivia removes the screwdriver. Olivia and Kris stare at each other, with fear-ladened eyes, heavy breathing, and two dead bodies at their feet, one grinning with a hole in his head, the other a lumbering pin cushion.

12

◇

Back at the convenience store…

Mike stands over Jimbo's body as the noise from the gunshot still rings in his ears. His eyes wince as he tries to shake it off, but being concussed from earlier in the evening surely isn't helping. His eyes open slowly, struggling to focus as he looks around and moves, it's like he sees things at a slower frame rate. He isn't processing things as fast as they happen, like watching a movie but the audio is delayed by a second. Mike stands there trying to collect himself for a moment longer and when he looks down at Jimbo he is disgusted by what he sees. His head, shot at point blank range with a sawed-off shotgun; so it looks exactly how one might imagine - like a baked potato dipped in spaghetti sauce that someone threw as hard as they could against the floor.

Mike loses his stomach onto the floor instantly. He hunches over, spitting and wiping his mouth as his heart races and his breathing is out of control. "Oh God," he breathes in between spitting. Mike walks around the counter, puts his back against the coolers, slides down the door, and sits on the floor as he looks at Jimbo's body. With his back against the glass, knees bent, he clutches the shotgun as he tries to control his breathing.

This certainly is not how Mike expected to be spending his summer break. He hadn't even made it home yet and he's killed someone. He found himself in a life or death situation that was very real and he had to decide quickly who should live. There is no time for mental gymnastics or justification as tears stream from his eyes as he sits there. Guilt weighs heavy on his mind while he stares at Jimbo's body on the floor of this backwoods truckstop shop. *What was Jimbo's life like, aside from being a complete lunatic?* Mike wondered. *Did he have a wife? Children? What if he has grandchildren?* "I'm sorry," he whispers, sobbing.

Mike wipes his face and tries to collect himself. He closes his eyes, leans his head back, and takes quick inhales, and lets out slow exhales. As he is performing this meditation exercise he quickly opens his eyes and realizes someone must have heard that gunshot. He springs to his feet and puts his back to every wall as he keeps his eyes on the front entrance and windows, like in every action movie he has ever watched when someone navigates a room with a gun. As he approaches the front door, he hears a scuffle in the parking lot. He goes to the window but cannot see anything.

Mike readies his gun and slowly starts to make his way to the door. He can hear laughter coming from the lot. Mike stands near the doorway, looking out through the broken glass, waiting to see if anyone is coming. With his heart racing, and being more scared than he's ever been in his life, he goes out the door and goes around to the other side of the gas station. He tries to be sneaky and not make any noise, keeping to the shadows along the side of the building that is opposite the lot.

As he creeps within the shadows, he hears a man grunting and yelling. Not long after, he hears what sounds like Olivia, and she is screaming. He tries to remain unseen and unheard as he creeps around the building. Tall grass and weeds block his view of what's going on behind the building. He gets closer to the weeds and looks through and sees the dumpster behind the building and sees Greaseball's body on the ground and Olivia on his back, pulling the screwdriver out of his head. He sees Kris standing there with a crowbar, leaning over and trying to catch his breath. Mike remains hidden for the now and just watches his friends.

Kris looks at Olivia and holds out his fist for her to bump it. "That was awesome!" he says through him catching his breath.

Olivia bumps it reluctantly. "We have to go. Right now!"

Kris looks at her a little puzzled. "Nah, we gotta find Mike."

"Mike ran to the front of the store. I think he might have gone inside," Olivia offers.

"We can't just leave him, Liv." Kris shrugs at Olivia,

She stares at Kris, waiting for the next move. "Well, what do we do Kris?"

"We need to take out as many of these fuckers as we can," he answers.

Olivia looks at Kris with concern. "Kris, no. We have to get the hell out of here. I can't do this. I can't, I can't," Olivia repeats with her voice breaking, shaking her head, on the verge of tears.

Kris places his hand on her shoulder and looks in her eyes. "It's gonna be alright. I got this. We got this," he assures.

He turns away from her and walks toward the barn with his arms spread out. "Where y'all at now? You motherfuckers wanna play games?" Kris shouts. "Come on! … I got one of yours!"

Olivia shuffles toward the cars and puts a little distance between her and Kris. "Kris! Stop! Come on! Let's get out of here, please!" she says in a loud whisper.

Kris spins around and looks at her as he walks backwards now, arrogantly, with the barn at his back. "I got one of yours! Come do somethin' bout it you bitches!" Kris shouts even louder. Kris turns, walking to the barn and he bangs on a picnic table with the crowbar. The sound of the wood knocking, echoes. "Come on out, let's see wha–" As Kris is pacing toward the barn and yelling he is struck through the back of his head with a bolt. Kris stumbles before plummeting forward, crumbling like a decaying, hollow redwood in a windstorm.

Olivia shrieks in horror and immediately covers her mouth and backs up between two cars near the grass. She looks to her left and sees Cliff, slinging the crossbow over his shoulder, walking over to Kris' body. Mike is still hidden on the other side of the gas station building, looking through the weeds, with the shotgun. Mike looks on in disbelief as he witnesses Kris be shot in the back of the head. Mike looks for Olivia but she is no longer in his sight.

"Yeeeeaaaah buddy!" Cliff says playfully as he pulls the bolt out of Kris' head. "Woooo! Fuckin' bullseye motherfuckers! …Anybody see that shit?" Cliff wipes the tip of the bolt on his jeans and puts it back onto the underside of his crossbow. "My God, I hope someone was filming that shit! Please tell me somebody caught that! …I need to talk to Bobby 'bout security cameras, get me one of them highlight tapes or some shit. WOO!" Cliff crouches down and rolls Kris over and looks at his face. The bolt went through the back of Kris' head and out of his left eye. "God damn! Bonus points! Yes!" Cliff declares, quite arrogantly, standing up and doing a celebratory fist pump. "That's what I call an eye for an eye you son of a bitch!"

Cliff looks around and he locks eyes with Olivia who is standing between two junked vehicles, watching as Kris is treated like a freshly killed deer. Cliff fixates on her, he sees nobody else in the lot and begins slowly walking to her. "Well hello little lady." Olivia backs into the unkempt grass and weeds that are behind the cars.

"Stay the fuck back!" Olivia threatens as she points the bloody and rusted screwdriver at Cliff.

Cliff gestures with his arms wide open and a smirk. "Awww honey. That little child's tool ain't gonna help you."

"I said stay back!" Olivia hisses.

"You're not still upset about your little boyfriend back in the barn, are you? Mister college superstar quarterback… Mister big fuckin' mouth, not enough brains for his hard fuckin' skull! That's behind us I would've thought. Why don't we start over… Hmm?" Cliff mocks.

"Don't you talk about him!" Olivia seethed.

Cliff continues to take small steps closer. "Oh, but did you see that badass bow shot I just did? Please tell me you did,"

Olivia backs away, and sees that it's nothing but tall grass and overgrown fields for a while and she thinks about making a run for it.

"You know, I might take off his head. Have it stuffed. My buddy Virgil, he does taxidermy and all sorts of wild shit. He can probably even make a new eye and you wouldn't know any better."

Olivia's backward walking turns to more of a faster side shuffle, as Cliff is coming at her with a normal pace.

"Or maybe I'll take your boyfriend's head. Have Virgil sew up that little cut in his forehead. Mount that shit right in my living room. How's that sound sweetie?"

Olivia's emotions take over when Cliff mentions her boyfriend. "I said not to fucking talk about him!" she screams as she lunges at Cliff and tries to stab him with the screwdriver. Cliff side steps her and grabs her waist and body slams her. She drops the screwdriver and now is fighting him while on her back. Cliff reaches for her arms as she is throwing punches and he is able to restrain her.

"So tell me how you want it. You want me to make it quick, or do you prefer I take my time?" Cliff laughs as Olivia is resisting desperately.

"LET HER GO, ASSHOLE!" Mike demands, with the shotgun aimed at Cliff. Cliff stands up and turns around. "Slowly!" Mike orders, tightening his aim right at Cliff's face as Cliff shows his hands.

13

◇

"Whoa, whoa, whoa, calm down, easy there cowboy," Cliff pleads, with careful movements. "You gonna shoot a man who has his hands up? Maybe we can work something out. Whuddaya say?" Cliff suggests, taking soft, gingerly steps toward Mike.

Olivia gets to her feet and takes a few steps away from Cliff and looks over at Mike. "Mike! Shoot this motherfucker!" she screams.

"Stay right there motherfucker!" Mike insists with authority as he takes a step closer with the gun raised at Cliff's head. Cliff stops in his tracks.

"Do it now Mike! KILL HIM!" Olivia screams.

Cliff looks back at Olivia and winks at her. "Don't look at her, I'm the one with the gun, eyes over here!" Mike says. Cliff looks back at Mike, and now takes a step back. "I said don't move!" Mike repeats.

"Mike! Pull the trigger! We have to get out of here! Please!" Olivia begs through tears.

Mike presses the gun to Cliff's chin, hesitant. "Olivia. Run. NOW!" Mike commands.

Olivia watches eager for Mike to pull the trigger, "I need to see you do it. This guy is bad–"

"OLIVIA! JUST GO! OKAY?" Mike interrupts.

Cliff jerks his head from the barrel of the gun and shoves Mike's arm, pushing the gun away from him. Cliff drives his knee into Mike's ribs and punches him in the face. Mike stumbles after taking the hit and swings around, pointing the gun at Cliff. Cliff charges at Mike, full speed, yelling and tackling him to the ground before he can even react. Cliff drops another punch into Mike's face, but Mike is able to hit Cliff in the nose with the stock of the gun and push him off with an explosive kick to his midsection. Cliff falls back, holding his mouth after getting hit.

"For fuck's sake! Did you have to hit me in the damn teeth?" Cliff cries out. Mike scrambles to his feet, aims the gun and squeezes the trigger only for it to make a clicking noise. No loud gunshot came from the business end of the shotgun this time. Mike failed to reload the shells after he fired it earlier.

Mike's expression matches his speech "Oh fuck!"

Cliff braces for the killshot until he hears the click of an unloaded gun and then looks relieved. "Oh you done fucked up big time son." Cliff comes toward Mike but Mike doesn't allow him to make the first move. Mike holds the gun like it's a baton, comes at Cliff head on, and throws a massive uppercut swing with the stock of the gun. Cliff moves and grabs Mike's arm and bends his wrist, putting his palm against the back of his shoulder in a position to break Mike's arm. Mike drops the gun and Cliff kicks it away. Cliff drives his foot into the back of Mike's legs causing him to fall onto his knees, and Cliff forces him face down onto the ground by controlling his arm.

Olivia walks over with her eyes on the gun. Cliff looks up at her quickly. "Honey, you take one more goddamn step and I swear to fuckin' Christ I'll rip his damn arm off right here!"

Olivia freezes, uncertain of what to do. She feels compelled to help, but knows she should run, but knows that Cliff will kill Mike, and he did just save her. She is conflicted on what to do but refuses to just watch this happen. Cliff twists Mike's arm and pins it to his back and leans down with his face close to Mike's. "I'm gonna kill you, and your little friend right there is gonna watch *all* of her friends die." Mike struggles, but Cliff is on top of him applying pressure and twisting more. "And then she's gonna die… it's gonna be nice and slow," Cliff growls into Mike's ear intimately, as to not let Olivia hear him.

Mike scoots his knees up close to his stomach and makes a last ditch effort to give everything he has to get Cliff off of him. Cliff tries to restrain Mike, but Mike is able to nearly get to his feet and create enough momentum to catch Cliff off guard. Olivia sees her opportunity and runs up behind Cliff, and puts her hands over his eyes, and digs her fingernails into his skin as she pulls him away from Mike. Cliff lets out a painful scream and immediately lets Mike go. He grabs Olivia's hands, overpowering her pretty easily, and throws them off of him. He steps away, as he feels around his face and the skin where she left deep scratches. He looks at his hands and sees blood and becomes furious. "You little…"

"Go! Now! Run!" Mike shouts at Olivia.

Cliff puts his hands up, ready to fight, staring at Mike through scratched eyes and blood. Mike keeps himself between Olivia and Cliff, and stands ready for anything. Cliff takes a few steps toward Mike and throws a jab. Mike smacks his hand away. Olivia runs off into the tall grass behind the junked cars.

Mike watches Cliff's movements and sees that he must have been a boxer at some point in his life because he is bobbing his head and moving like a trained fighter in the ring. Cliff comes in closer and throws another shot with his left hand at Mike's midsection and as Mike blocks that soft blow, Cliff rains down a right hook to his jaw. Mike falls back, stunned. Cliff walks over to Mike as he is scuffling to get to his feet. Cliff feels his face, still bleeding, looks to his right, and spits blood onto the ground. Mike backs away and is holding his jaw, and opening his mouth to see if he can still open and close it. Cliff gets back in the fighting stance, and is moving a little faster now.

"Better stick and move, kid. Next one knocks you out," Cliff brags arrogantly.

Mike feels around his pockets and feels where he has the pocket knife that he took from the gas station still. Mike does not go for the knife, he wants to keep the fight to his advantage and find his moment.

Cliff steps to him and throws another shot to the midsection and Mike jumps back. Cliff throws an opposite hand jab and Mike steps aside and sticks his leg out, tripping Cliff, sending him to the ground as Mike quickly reaches for the pocket knife and opens it. Mike rushes at Cliff as he is trying to quickly get back to his feet.

"AAAARGH!" Mike rushes him from the side and buries the knife into the right side of Cliff's abdomen. Mike yanks the knife, and the teeth on the blade chew on his flesh and the muscle underneath. The blade is caught on skin as Mike looks Cliff in the eyes, face to face. Cliff lets out a scream instantly. Mike then tugs on the knife, desperately trying to pull it out, and it jerks

Cliff closer to him. In the process he has opened Cliff up pretty good. It is about an 8 inch wide, jagged slice that's pouring blood now. Mike pulls as hard as he can, and Cliff matches the same amount of effort to just pull away. With Cliff pulling at the same time as Mike, Cliff lets out the most gut-wrenching, uneasy yelp that Mike has ever heard before. The knife comes free from all of the force and Cliff falls to the dirt, holding his stomach.

Hyperventilating, Mike looks around, as he grips the knife and it is completely covered in Cliff's blood, as is his hand. Mike doesn't see Olivia anywhere around. He looks to the barn and sees a couple of people come out and start jogging to him.

Cliff holds onto his stomach from the ground, and he is thrashing about in agonizing pain. "You motherfucker! You son of a bitch! You fucking cut me! You really fucking got me! Ow, shit!"

Mike sees the others coming and he runs in the direction that Olivia ran off in. He runs between the cars, and sprints into the grass, and disappears into the darkness.

As Cliff throws his fit on the ground, thrashing about writhing in pain, Ozzy and two other women get to him in a hurry. Ozzy stops and sees Kris' body, Greaseball and Buck's as well. It's a horrific mess in the dirt lot, right out in the open.

"He fucking got me Oz! He got me real fuckin' good. Ahhhh!" Cliff cries. "Help me Ozzy! Please!" The two women run to Cliff's aid. One woman asks him to lie back and relax. "It hurts!" he cries.

The woman puts her hand on his face to comfort him "I know, but –" as she touches his face he tenses up more.

"Ahhhh! That bitch tore up my face!" The two women look at one another with looks that say, without words, that this isn't good.

Ozzy kneels down at Cliff's side. "Brother... I'm not gonna sugarcoat it. It doesn't look good."

Cliff looks up to Ozzy with annoyance. "Well fuckin' hell Oz, it don't feel good either!"

One of the women looks at Cliff. "Brother. I need to move your hand and get a better look."

The other woman holds Cliff's hand and speaks calmly. "Just breathe sweetie."

Cliff moves his hand and the other woman covers her mouth in awe of just how bad it is. Ozzy sees it as well and shakes his head. Cliff's intestines are literally falling out and he was trying to keep his innards inside of his body.

Patty comes out of the grass and sees people crowding around and she rushes over. She is so focused on the hunt that she doesn't notice the bodies on the ground. She sees Cliff in Ozzy's arms and before she could ask questions, Ozzy looks at Patty and gestures to the grass behind the cars. "There are two of them. The girl and one of the guys. They ran off. Find them!" Patty nods and without hesitation heads into the grass and further into the darkness.

The woman holding Cliff's hand continues to speak calmly to him. "Everything is gonna be alright hun. Just rest."

Ozzy looks to the two women and takes a deep breath and sighs. "Why don't you two head on back? Tell a few of the guys to come out and clean this shit up," Ozzy suggests, gesturing to the 3 bodies behind them in the lot.

"Yes Ozzy," the two women acknowledge him and walk off.

Ozzy grabs Cliff's hand in a brotherly way and leans in close to him. "Cliff. You're my brother."

Cliff begins to cry as he looks Ozzy in the eyes. "You're my brother Ozzy."

Ozzy looks away, fighting back tears, then turns back to Cliff who is beginning to sob harder with each second. "You've always been my brother. You always will be. You know that, don'tcha?"

Ozzy begins to get a little choked up with his words as he watches Cliff go from being a formidable badass to a sobbing baby, waiting to die. "I know Oz. I know."

"I love you brother. God's gonna be so good to you. He's gonna be waiting with open arms. And you know what? He's gonna thank you Cliff. He's gonna thank you for all the good you've done. All the cleansing you've done in His name, for his world. He's gonna be so glad to have you by His side finally." Ozzy begins to break down during his speech.

Cliff cries uncontrollably and has completely let go now. "I did everything you ever asked me Oz! I love you too… I… Love you so much."

Ozzy looks Cliff in the eyes with compassion for his brother. "I'm not gonna let you suffer. You know that right?"

Cliff cries aloud, "It should be you. It has to be you. Tell everyone I love them, and I will be waiting for them, by His side."

Ozzy smiles through tears and nods. "I will tell them brother. Thank you for being a brother, and a friend." Ozzy reaches around his back and unclicks a snap button that holds a buck knife and he slowly removes it from the sheath on his belt. He leans forward and kisses Cliff on his forehead. "Go there, God is waiting," and he plunges the knife into Cliff's temple, killing him quickly. The crying and sobbing ends.

Ozzy holds onto the handle and hangs his head down, somber, before he removes the knife as gently as he can, and wipes the blood off on Cliff's shirt. From his knees, Ozzy sits for a moment staring at Cliff. He has a moment to think about everything he has done that has led to this point, and what needs to happen next. He has never lost people before… not like this, this is new. Ozzy rises to his feet, dusts himself off, and he walks over to Greaseball and Buck's bodies lying in the dirt.

"You boys didn't deserve this. May you serve God at His side, take care of each other," he says as he motions his fingers in the shape of a cross on his chest. He inspects how they were likely killed wearing a tense scowl on his face, pacing around their bodies with a lot of energy, frustration and nowhere to direct it.

Ozzy heads back to the barn and sees people standing in the doorway waiting for him to return. Three men are heading out. One has a wheelbarrow while the others have shovels and water jugs. Ozzy walks intently and passes the guys without so much as looking at them. Ozzy is overcome with anger that not even he is familiar with, a blind rage that must be directed productively, to avenge his fallen brothers.

14

◇

Olivia's feet move one after the other, faster than they probably ever have at any point in her life. No amount of caffeine can fuel this level of energy, intensity, and adrenaline. With her heart racing as fast as her legs, Olivia has run all out through the fields, and through patches of woods, without looking back for several minutes. This is an all out effort to get as far away as she can but now she is starting to slow down and physically become unable to continue at this pace. She eventually comes to a stop and she looks behind her for the first time. She sees nothing and is relieved. She leans forward and rests her hands on her knees as she lowers her head to try and breathe before going back into a lighter jog. Her breathing and wheezing sing along with the crickets and the occasional owl. Her jog eventually slows and she just walks ahead. She looks behind her every ten seconds or so, paranoid, expecting someone to be chasing her. There is no one, just the silence of the night smothering her. Darkness is cast from the trees, and moonlight breaks through minimally.

Olivia has no idea how far she has run but has moved in this direction for a bit now. As she marches on and her breathing becomes normal again, she thinks about everything she just witnessed in that short time. She thinks about how different her night has gone compared to what she had planned. Summer break should mean a break from stress, time with friends and family, time to catch up on the things she is wanting to do without the worry of deadlines and classes. She thinks about Nathan and how they should be cuddled up on a couch somewhere right now having fun together, laughing, possibly a little buzzed, and just enjoying life. The future and how her ideas of a happy life are ruined. Tears break through and she looks back, to find nothing.

She thinks about Kris and how close they were as longtime friends, and how close Kris and Nathan were, long before she ever came into the picture. She thinks about where Mike is and if something bad happened after she ran. She is sick to her stomach that something bad probably happened and that it was her fault somehow. Olivia's mind is racing and all over the place with erratic thinking. *Who are these people that did this? What kind of monsters would take something this far?* She is not able to focus and compartmentalize everything at this time. Fight or flight has kicked in and with her life at stake, she does not have the luxury of processing these thoughts and feelings, only surviving.

Olivia thinks about her family. She hasn't even gotten to visit them yet. She had plans to do that in the morning. Her mother, father, and younger sister were going to take her out to breakfast and talk about school and everything they have going on. It was going to be nice. Now she wonders how she will tell her family about what happened, or if she will even get to. She looks behind her once more.

The image of Nathan looking up at Ozzy just before he drops the ax replays in her mind, seared into her brain. When she closes her eyes, the memory is even clearer. The sound of Kris yelling and knowing how bad that must have hurt Kris to watch it happen, compounded with the overpowering feeling of complete and utter helplessness, weighs heavy on her. If Olivia escapes, she wonders if she will tell the police or if Ozzy was serious about what would happen if she did. She thinks about the gas station interaction earlier with the woman. The woman just stared at her with no smiles, no attitude, or any expression whatsoever. She spoke to her with a deep and almost strained voice and was just an intense person to be around. *How many people are out here looking for us?*

With so many thoughts in Olivia's head as she walks through the darkness, alone and scared, she realizes she has been walking parallel to the road this whole time. She looks behind her to find no one. She makes her way closer to the road, into a more open, and welcoming area, and sees nothing. The faded and forgotten stretch of road goes straight for as far as she can see. She walks in the patches of grass and is visibly exhausted. Her legs are weak and her feet feel heavy with each step she takes. Her arms hang, swinging, and her face is dirty and soiled with dried tears. Everything about her stride and body language looks like that of a zombie.

She continues to look behind her with paranoia and fear seeded deeply. It's not even a thought, it's an involuntary action now. There is a band of God-pleasing killers somewhere looking for her right now and the darkness is not doing her any favors. The singular goal is to just get as far away as possible and survive. She has walked for what feels like forever, her feet drag through the dirt. She keeps her eyes forward, watching with a look of defeat on her face until she sees a glimmer in the distance, focusing as the glimmer becomes brighter. It's a car, oncoming from the opposite direction of the barn, heading right toward her. She becomes very alert again as she plays out the scenario in her head and decides if she should wave them down or try to hide.

Olivia anticipates the car getting closer and has to make a decision fast. She looks at the grass and considers getting face down on her stomach and waiting until the car passes. If she lies down and hides the car will pass and no one will ever know she was there and she can just keep walking. If she tries to stop them though it could be one of those crazy old people who she is specifically trying to avoid. Maybe they're patrolling the road. Then again, she is in need of help and this could be that only chance at help. After all, they are coming from the opposite direction.

Olivia rationalizes the possibilities and decides to try and flag them down. Olivia takes a few steps into the road and walks toward the oncoming headlights, hoping that it might be a good samaritan. Olivia raises her hand high and tries to be seen. The car is still far away and the road is not lit like the roads in the city are. She waves around hoping they will stop for a strange girl on the side of the road late at night, despite the stigma that horror movies have created. The last person who stopped to help her on the side of the road ended up chaining her up and driving her to her boyfriend's execution. She is hopeful that this is the break she needs so desperately right now.

The car approaches and it slows down. Olivia notices and thinks they might see her. The car drives closer and the headlights are bright. Olivia puts her arm over her eyes and tries to make out the person inside, standing in the road unable to see much, but hears the tires crunching over gravel slower, as the car comes to a stop. The person rolls the driver side window down and leans his head out. "Hey, are you alright?" the stranger asks.

Olivia walks out of the light and to the side of the car to get a better look at the driver. It is a younger man, probably not much older than her. He is driving a newer model car, unlike anything back at the barn. It's silver and pretty ordinary looking. Olivia is unsure what to say, in fear of saying too much and spooking her possible savior.

"Are you hurt? Do you need help?" he asks.

Olivia hesitates and looks behind her again.

The man picks up on her nervous behavior and can tell something terrible has happened. "What's your name? Do you need me to call someone, or take you somewhere?"

"My name is Olivia. I– I need a hospital," Olivia stutters.

15

◇

"Olivia. My name is Tom." He offers, looking her up and down, noticing how rough of shape she is in. "What happened to you?"

Olivia looks at Tom with despair in her eyes. "There are these… people. Th-They're looking for me. They killed my friends. Now they're trying to kill me," she explains, feeling like she has already said too much to this stranger.

Tom looks at her shocked. "Okay, okay, okay, just calm down." Tom turns off his car and steps out. Tom is dressed business casual with a collared t-shirt, khakis, nice haircut, very unassuming and most likely not part of that band of old people up the road. He doesn't even have a southern accent. Olivia looks around nervously as Tom pulls out his phone. "Ugh, this is just great. No signal. I hate driving in the middle of nowhere." Tom looks at Olivia. "I am not getting any signal–"

"Listen. I need you to take me far away from here. Please!" Olivia interrupts.

Tom looks at the ground for a second, and puts his thumb and index finger across his eyebrows. "Look, I'm not…." Tom sees a man run out of the grass with a lot of blood on him. "Whoa! Whoa! Whoa! Is that one of them?" Tom jumps back, ready to hop back into the car and burn rubber. "Get back!"

Olivia looks back alarmed but with great relief sees it's Mike. "Olivia!" Mike shouts as he runs to her.

'Mike! You're alive!" Olivia runs to Mike and they hug each other tight, so tight that they may never let go of one another again. "I thought they were going to kill you." Olivia whispers.

Mike pulls away looking at Olivia. "I am so happy I caught up to you. I was so worried something might have happened."

Tom stands there watching awkwardly. "Um… Hey, you guys… Someone mind telling me what's going on? Is this a prank or something? Is anyone else about to come out and tell me I'm on Youtube or somethin'?"

Mike goes over to Tom. "Listen. Sir. Please. You have got to take us up the road. The way you came from. You don't want to go down this road. Trust me."

Tom backs up and is in a defensive position. "Hold on man. I need to know what's going on before I just let a scared woman and a man who came out of the woods covered in blood into my car with me at night. I'm starting to wonder why I even stopped now that I'm thinking about it."

Olivia looks at Tom with tears in her eyes. "Because you're a decent person Tom… Please?"

Tom puts his hands on his waist and looks up the road. He pulls his keys out of his pocket and swings them around his finger. "Alright. I'll take you up the road. But I think you both should go to a hospital and get che–"

"Tom, get in the fuckin' car!" Olivia shrieks as she sees Patty come out of the trees, holding the large, curved knife and wearing her creepy mask as she stops and stares on the side of the road.

Tom looks confused at Olivia. Mike yells at Tom. "She's behind you! Get in the car! Now!" Tom turns around and sees Patty walking at him quickly with murder in her eyes.

"Oh shit!" Tom yells as he races over to his car and gets in, shuts the door and is fumbling his keys.

Mike hops in the front seat and Olivia in the back. Mike and Olivia are both yelling at Tom. "Come on, hurry! Drive!" Patty walks over to the car and smacks the driver side window with her palm.

"Oh fuck! Fuck! Fuck! Fuck!" Tom gets the key in the ignition and starts it up, and mashes the gas pedal. Patty takes a swing at the car with the knife and busts the back driver side window as Tom speeds off. Olivia puts her arms up to shield her face from the glass shattering.

The three speed away as Tom looks in the rearview mirror and sees Patty standing in the road holding the large knife, with her mask on watching them get away. "What in the fuck is going on?" Tom yells as he jerks on the steering wheel. "That lady busted my window!"

"We're sorry. I swear, you get us somewhere safe, I will buy you so many new windows," Mike says, feeling guilty for getting this stranger involved in this madness.

Olivia leans forward, from the back. "Yeah. We will make this right. We're just thankful you stopped. I know how this must look."

Tom is white-knuckling the steering wheel. "So who-who the hell even was that lady? Di- did you tell me that some people *KILLED* your friends?" Tom asks, stumbling over his tongue.

"There are some *really* bad people up this way. We should turn around and go the other way," Olivia urges.

"I'm– I'm sorry. Wait a minute. So these people killed your friends. And now they're trying to kill you?" Tom asks, trying to understand the situation.

"That's right," Mike replies.

"And now I'm wrapped up in this bullshit too?" Tom yells.

"We just need to keep moving. We should turn around though," Mike warns.

"What was that mask she was wearing?" Tom asks, with his voice rattled.

"What happened back there? After I ran? Are you okay?" Olivia asks Mike.

"I'm alright. I'm just happy I found you out there," Mike tells her.

"So, this lady is just chasing you with a big knife through fields late at night?" Tom questions.

Olivia sits in silence for a moment, ignoring Tom and feeling the night air blow into the backseat from the busted window.

"What about the guy? With the crossbow?" she asks.

"What guy with a crossbow?" Tom asked, even more panicked.

Mike stares out the window, thinking of the right way to put her mind at ease. "He's not going to be a problem now," Mike sighs and looks back at her. "But there were others that came just before I ran. I saw an opening and took off."

Olivia leans back into the seat and closes her eyes for a moment. Mike looks around anxiously for the gas station. Tom contains his freak-out with his eyes fixed to the road and his foot on the gas.

"Hey man, slow down a little. I think that gas station is up ahead," Mike says.

"No way man. Slow down? Are you kidding me? Why would anyone slow down right now?" Tom asks.

"Our friend's car broke down a few miles from this gas station and someone pulled over to help us. He was one of these people," Mike explains. "You have got to turn around. I don't know what we're driving into."

Tom looks over to Mike as he presses the gas a little more. The engine hums a little louder. "Just relax pal. I got this."

Mike sees that Tom isn't going to listen at this point. Fear has taken the wheel as Tom is in fight or flight mode, and his body has chosen flight. Mike feels under the seat frantically. He finds nothing so he reaches for the glove box. He starts pulling papers out and ransacking Tom's car from the passenger seat.

"Whoa. Hey! What do you think you're doing?" Tom asks angrily.

"Do you have any weapons in this car? Preferably a gun?" Mike asks, shuffling through Tom's things.

Tom's eyes go wider as he looks back at the road. "I'm a twenty-four-year-old underwriter at a bank. What the hell would I be doing with a gun?" he responds, with surprise in his voice.

"What about in the trunk? Do you have any tools? Something man. We need to protect ourselves!" Mike shouts.

Mike carelessly stuffs all of the papers and disheveled first aid kit back into the glove box and slams it shut. He fixes his eyes out the window and tries to focus, becoming noticeably afraid. "That's it, up there!" Mike sees the dimly lit reader board way up the road. It casts the only light you can see. "Dude. We need to turn this car around, man. Seriously!"

Olivia becomes very alert as Mike raises his voice and sees the gas station readerboard, like it's the only star in the sky beyond the car's bright headlights. "Tom. Please stop. You have to turn around right now," Olivia cries.

Tom smacks the steering wheel, and he puts a little bass in his voice. "I'M NOT STOPPING! DO YOU UNDERSTAND ME?"

As they speed down the road and come closer to the gas station, Mike sees brake lights backing out quickly. He sees Virgil's pick up truck with the wrecker. It's backing up at full speed out of that dirt path that leads to the barn.

"That's them! In the truck!" Mike points. Olivia braces herself, grabbing onto the driver seat and passenger seat headrests.

Tom continues to speed and sees that this truck isn't slowing down. Tom speeds up to pass it. "I hope you guys put on your seat belts. Hold on!"

Mike puts on his seat belt. Olivia does as well. "Come on, come on, go! Go!" Mike roars.

Tom tenses up as they barrel closer toward this oncoming truck. Tom is going as fast as the car will let him go. "Shit! Shit! SHIT!" As they are just about to pass the truck that is quickly backing out of the driveway, Tom swerves into the other lane to just barely avoid smashing head first into the back of the truck, but the truck backs into the car, clipping it as it passes, causing it to tailspin past the gas station altogether and off of the road into some overgrown fields. The tires screech like they're singing a quartet after the crash just before they are slowed by the tall grass on the roadside. The rubber from the tires paint sloppy black lines on the battered pavement as the car dances off of the road. The car spins around several times before coming to a complete stop and the three inside are visibly jarred.

16

◇

Tom unbuckles his seatbelt and is breathing heavily, possibly having a panic attack as he opens the door and falls out onto the ground. Mike sits there for a second, and tries to shake off the dizziness a bit. He sees Tom hop out of the car pretty quickly. The sounds around him are fuzzy and muffled.

"Mike!" Olivia opens the door and shakes him as he stares at Tom, spaced out. "MIKE!" she screams. Mike slowly turns to Olivia and sees the urgency in her face. "Come on! We gotta go Mike!"

He takes off the seatbelt, leans out of the car, and falls face first onto the ground. Olivia grabs his arm and tries her best to bring him to his feet. Mike plants his knee into the dirt and rises to his feet. He stands up and feels a pain in his neck as he is looking around. He reacts to the pain and Olivia can see it in his face that he is hurt. He opens his eyes and sees Tom coming over to them. He sees the car smoking and the headlights shining bright, but blocked by the tall grass brushing against the hood of the car. He looks toward the road and sees the truck sitting there still as the emergency lights flash. Tom is talking to Olivia, inaudible to Mike at all. He looks at Tom who is shaking him and snapping his finger in Mike's face. Mike closes his eyes really hard for a second and shakes it off and everything speeds up and the present hits him. He can hear again.

"Can you hear me? Anybody in there? Hey! HEY!" Tom shouts at Mike.

Mike nods. "Yeah, yeah, I'm good. Come on." Mike walks into the grass away from the road. Olivia and Tom follow. Tom runs ahead of them.

"I'm sorry guys. I can't die here," Tom says, sprinting ahead.

Olivia starts to lightly jog and fires a look back at Mike. "You've gotta move Mike, we've gotta keep going, They're coming!"

Mike begins to lightly jog, trying to match Olivia's pace practically dragging his leg along as he fights through the pain. "I'm coming. I'm coming. You go ahead of me if you have to." Mike insists.

Olivia slows down to stay with Mike. "I'm not leaving you. We've been through too much to just die now. You have to push through this." Olivia tries her best to keep Mike moving as she watches over her shoulder. No one can be seen coming for them and they have gotten far away from the road and the crash. The problem now is that they are deep in tall grass, stalks of corn and sunflowers and have lost visibility in all directions.

"Where is that guy at?" Mike asks.

"He took off. I'm not sure. We have to worry about each other right now," Olivia sputters.

Mike and Olivia move through the tall stalks, making a lot of noise as they do. Dry leaves rustling against them as they pass through, the snapping and crackling of the stems breaking with each step. Mike struggles to keep up. Olivia sees a clearing ahead and they push through to get to it. They're far from the road now, but have no sense of direction. The clearing is wide enough for a tractor and it looks to have been done recently, made up of flattened brush, grass, and packed dirt makeup this clearing. Olivia looks to her right and sees that it goes to the road. She looks to her left and sees hills in the distance under the dark night sky. Mike stops and hunches over, trying to catch his breath.

Olivia grabs Mike's arm and pulls him toward her. "Come on. We have to get off this path. They'll see us."

Mike comes along, huffing and wheezing. "We have to find another way. We're making a lot of noises. They can probably hear us," he says through big exhales.

Olivia runs ahead and Mike continues, following along, slowing down a bit from the general exhaustion. They approach another clearing where two paths intersect. Olivia looks around and all directions look the same under the cover of darkness. Olivia runs to the left, and Mike follows. This path seems to go further from the road. The two make their way along the path when Mike sees the end.

"It looks like a yard up ahead," Mike wheezes between his winded breaths.

Olivia slows down and steps to the side, closer to the crops, but not into them, as to be stealthy. Mike does the same. The two now walk slowly and carefully to not make any noise, or cast shadows, until they know what is ahead. Olivia squints her eyes and looks across what looks to be a mowed pasture that goes for a while. Olivia leans her head out and looks around and doesn't see anyone or anything really. There are some trees spread out, but other than that it looks to be someone's property and they take care of it up to a certain point.

"What do you see?" Mike whispers.

Olivia hesitates before she answers. "It looks safe, but it's wide open… Could be dangerous if we are seen. Nowhere to go."

Mike steps to the other side of Olivia and pokes his head out now. He looks out to the vast open grass, and through the trees straight ahead. "I'm not sure, but I think I see a house out there." Mike points in the direction, hoping he is right and Olivia sees it too.

Olivia tries to focus and looks where Mike is pointing. "I think it might be," she says. She notices what looks like a silhouette of a house far across the yard. "What do you think?"

"About what?" Mike responds.

"The house… Should we see if someone is there?" Olivia asks.

Mike looks uneasy about the question. "Liv, I don't know. The last two times we tried to trust someone it went horribly wrong. What if these people aren't home because they're part of that cult?"

Olivia dramatically sighs. "But what if they aren't and it's just regular people?"

"What if we go knock on their door though and they're not happy about two strangers, covered in blood and dirt showing up in the middle of the night?" Mike asks.

"We've been running all night it feels like. Do you want to keep running all night? You're hurt and we're both scared," Olivia fires back.

Mike looks at Olivia, with an exhausted, albeit swollen expression. "I don't think we should risk it. We should keep moving."

Olivia takes a deep breath. She is not a fan of trekking through these fields and woods all night, but she begrudgingly agrees. "Fine, we will cut through this yard and move further from this road."

Mike nods with approval. "Alright. We'll use the trees to cover while we're moving through here."

Olivia nods. "Alright. Let's move." She says as she steps out into the yard moving quickly and crouching down low. Mike is right behind her and does the same. The smell of freshly mowed grass and mulch fill their nostrils as they hobble quickly to the first tree in the yard. They look around cautiously and everything is quiet. All of a sudden two gunshots ring out from the direction they had come from. Olivia and Mike stare at one another and try not to panic. They shuffle about twenty yards to the next tree quietly, trying to stick close to the trees as they stop. They look around and there are only crickets singing under the stars. They continue through the yard, zig-zagging from tree to tree until they get close enough to see the house and get an idea of what the situation is.

It's an old farmhouse. The windows have white frames that contrast the dark brown color. There is a large porch that wraps around the house, and stairs that lead up to it that are at least ten feet up from the yard. The two approach the house from what looks like the back yard. They continue to creep around, lying low, and moving with soft feet. Mike and Olivia start to make their way to the side of the house and try to stay out of the eyeline of the windows. As they are moving from one tree to the next, a bright motion-sensored flood light illuminates across the backyard. The light is blinding and shines on everything and makes Mike and Olivia *very* visible, and even more vulnerable.

Mike and Olivia stop in their tracks and hold their hands over their eyes and try to look ahead but are frozen. They hear a dog barking coming from the house. The bark is loud, feeling more like a roar echoing in the house, carrying into the night, demanding to be heard. Mike grabs Olivia by her arm. "Come on! Hide!" he says as they run to a carport that has multiple vehicles and some farming equipment.

As they're running, Olivia looks up and sees a dog jumping and barking at the window by the door. The bark gets louder and more ferocious as Olivia sees the dog. "I think the dog saw us," she says.

Mike hides and pulls Olivia into the carport and they sit against a riding mower, waiting to see if anyone is going to come out.

"Maybe they'll think it was a raccoon or a possum or something and just ignore it," Mike suggests, in an ever-so-hopeful tone.

Olivia watches the door anxiously as the dog continues to stir the noise. A light comes on upstairs in the house, and from outside they see shadows moving around the room. Shortly after, a light downstairs comes on. Mike watches quietly and still as the fear begins to sink in deeper. The anxiety, the anticipation of who is in that house, the discipline it takes to hide calmly and not take off sprinting is to be applauded. The door opens and a man holding a rifle stands in the doorway. The dog bursts out past his legs and down the staircase, like a lion getting the jump on a gazelle that it's been watching graze in a field. The dog blazes through the yard and is heading directly toward the carport.

"Shit!" Mike shouts, as he steps out with his hands up.

The man sees Mike and steps out onto his porch. He points the rifle and yells out to Mike from the top step, "I hope you got a good reason to be in my yard!"

17

◇

Earlier, before the crash…

Ozzy walks into the barn with his head held low. Everyone in the compound falls silent when he walks in. Ozzy is just moments removed from performing a mercy killing of his friend Cliff just outside. He walks by everyone, without acknowledging the quiet eyes on him. Those around him stand by watching and waiting for what Ozzy has to say, but he walks in visibly upset. Blood covers his hands, arms, and the front of his shirt. They move out of his way as his heavy feet create a symphony against the wooden floor. He heads straight into the bathroom and slams the door behind him, rattling the walls of the barn along with the bones of everyone staring at one another in silence when they hear an audible yell come from the bathroom. "AAAAGGGGHHHH!" Ozzy cries out.
Discomfort is heavy in the air with Ozzy's roar so emotionally charged that it could make God Himself tremble.

Some of the people begin to whisper amongst themselves. The two women who were outside with Ozzy and Cliff start to tell everyone that Cliff was killed and that Greaseball and Buck were as well. No one has seen Jimbo but they know he is out there so there is concern for him. Some begin to cry after hearing of the loss tonight. Buck, Cliff, and Greaseball were close to the community and there is an overwhelming sense of sadness at the moment.

Ozzy stands at the sink and places his hands along the front lip of the counter and leans on the sink with his arms outstretched and tensed up. He stares at the floor and raises his head to see his reflection in the mirror. There is blood on his face, and the front of his shirt is stained with blood, and the blood on his skin hasn't even dried yet. He leaves bloody handprints on the sink counter, stares into his own eyes in the mirror and has a moment of isolated thought. He breathes deeply through his nose, so hard that his face scrunches up with each inhale and his breaths become faster.

He impulsively strikes the mirror with his palm and cracks it. It's turned into a roadmap of cracked glass, splintering from edge to edge. He revisits his reflection through the cracked web and nothing but sadness, pain, and boiling anger stare back at him.

"I see you. You know what you have to do now," Ozzy says to himself, maintaining eye contact held with his broken reflection. "You have to do right by your brother. That's what he would want." His bottom lip sticks out as he frowns and shakes his head. "This wasn't how things were supposed to go. This wasn't part of the plan. No, no, no this was *NOT* part of the plan! This isn't supposed to happen to us. Not our people." He turns on the water and begins to rinse his hands and he looks down and watches the blood thin out and come off of his hands. Red streaks become pink and wash through his fingers as steam rises from the faucet. "I will make this right. They will not only pay for this, but they will suffer." His voice cracks as he becomes angrier and fights back tears. "They will suffer a wrath fitting of all their oppression, their complete lack of decency." Ozzy's frustration clouds his brain as he struggles to articulate. "Decency to, to, to their elders." He begins lathering his forearms with hand soap to clean up. He rinses his face and slicks his hair back, turns off the sink faucet, and looks himself in the mirror again as he heads back out.

Everyone turns their attention to Ozzy, and the whispers in the room fall silent. He looks over to one of the women who is crying and he walks up to her and offers his arms open wide. "Come on. It's okay," he says as he hugs the woman, burying her face into his chest as she loses it. She is bawling her eyes out. "That's it honey. Let it out," he consoles her like a close family member. After a moment, she pulls away and Ozzy walks away. He starts to take his shirt off as he is talking to the room. "So I take it you've all caught wind of what happened out there by now." He tosses his bloodied button down shirt on the floor and pulls a plain white t-shirt from a duffle bag sitting on a table. "Our brothers Buck, Cliff, and Greaseball... They– Well they didn't make it." As he says the names, several people weep in the room. The confirmation of the losses hit others like a suckerpunch. "Cliff, he died in my arms. I refused to let him suffer. I made it quick. He knew it was the right thing to do." Ozzy puts the shirt on. "It was difficult and I'm gonna have to carry that with me the rest of my days... But we are gonna have to pull together as a family, now more than ever, I'd say. We have to find these animals who did this and make sure that they don't escape, to protect our mission to God, and also to make sure they feel every ounce of pain that we're all feeling in this room right now." Ozzy slaps his chest. "Our internal pain will be theirs to feel soon enough! So we need to go out there, and hunt these heathens down. We must unleash the justice of an angel army!"

Ozzy looks around the room and begins to approach one of the men standing there. He pokes the man in the chest. "Wild Turkey! Virgil, my brother, you in?"

Virgil stares back intensely with a mouth full of tobacco. "Yep!"

Ozzy walks over to another guy. "What about you? Are you gonna stand by and let this kind of filth come in here and take apart your community?"

The man shakes his head no with total conviction. "No sir. Not this house."

"That's right!" Ozzy shouts. "Nobody should stand here idle tonight. We must go out there and find them and eradicate them from existence."

Ozzy goes over to Jasper, who stands there proudly with a tight grip on the neck of a hatchet. Jasper's eyes meet Ozzy's. "What are you gonna do? Cliff was our brother. You two were thick as thieves growing up," Ozzy says, sending a jolt through Jasper.

Jasper's face contorts while he tries to resist the anger he is feeling. "This is personal now Oz, I'm gonna hack those two into pieces and I'm gonna smile while doin' it," Jasper hissed.

Ozzy smirks in approval, placing a hand on Jasper's shoulder. "A man out for justice. Well let's go and get us some justice then."

Ozzy turns away and is walking across the floor as his walkie goes off. It's Patty's voice. "Homebase, do you have a copy? This is Chipmunk, over."

Ozzy grabs the walkie, "Go ahead Chipmunk, this is Homebase. What is your status? Over."

"I'm about two and half miles or so up the road. Our new friends got a ride from someone in a silver car. Busted window. They're inbound right now. Over."

Ozzy points to Jasper. "Keys are in Virgil's truck. We need to block the road right now. Go! Go! Go!"

Jasper jogs over to the truck and starts it up. He puts it into reverse, looks over his right shoulder, and starts to back up. As he is backing out, he sees a set of headlights coming down the road.

Ozzy walks out by the truck shouting into the window at Jasper, "That's THEM! GO!"

Jasper mashes the gas pedal and is going fast through the dirt lot, whizzing past all of the cars, and gas station, barreling in reverse into the road as the silver car tries to swerve around, clipping the truck, sending it spinning with the tires screeching before going into some tall crops on the other side of the road. Jasper is shaken by the impact but it is minimal compared to the car he clipped. He looks over the steering wheel and sees Ozzy and a couple others running to the truck. Jasper drives the truck slowly into the lot and puts it in park at the edge of the lot, turns the engine off and gets out.

"Jasper, you alright?" one of the men asks.

"I think so. I'm good, nothin' I can't walk off," Jasper assures, rotating his head around and stretching his neck.

Ozzy calls Patty over the radio. "Homebase to Chipmunk, do you copy?"

"Go for Chipmunk," Patty says.

"Your ride is enroute," Ozzy replies.

"Copy, over."

Ozzy goes over to a guy outside. "Hey Kenny. Do me a favor."

A tall slender man waits for Ozzy's request. "Whatcha need?"

Ozzy tosses a set of keys to Kenny. "About 2 miles up the road. Go scoop up Sister Patty. We'll wait here…"

Kenny nods and takes off for the car.

Ozzy charges past Jasper and into the road. He turns to the group. "Alright. We need a plan here. They're in that field and Jasper knocked 'em silly I'm sure. We're gonna have to be smart though. They're scrappy and we may have underestimated them. No more games. Get your weapons. We're gonna track em' down. And send em' to God. The girl, if we can keep her alive though, we can still attempt The Cleansing again." Kenny drives past them, in a beat up Chevy Malibu, and takes a left turn out of the lot. "I need a few guys to patrol the main road. They might come creepin' out and we can't afford to let them get away." Virgil is heading back to the barn to get prepared. "Ay, Virgil!" Ozzy hollers.

"Yeah, boss?" Virgil shouts back.

"Grab my pistol, would ya?"

"You got it."

Ozzy stands around, pacing anxiously. He stares out to the field across the street and watches the thrashed part of the tall grass where the car drove through after the wreck. A few minutes pass until Virgil comes hustling back to meet Ozzy at the road.

The men stand around for a moment as Kenny pulls into the lot and parks. Patty steps out of the car and comes over to Ozzy. Patty takes a look around and sees blood in the dirt and Ozzy looking a bit on-edge. "What the hell happened Oz?"

Ozzy hugs Patty tight and whispers into her ear, "They killed our brothers."

Patty pulls away from the embrace and stares at Ozzy a little puzzled, bracing herself for bad news. "…Who?"

Ozzy pauses, as he tries to not get choked up. "They got Buck, Cliff, and Greaseball. They're gone."

Patty turns around and tears up with her back to everyone.

"They fuckin' killed our people! Like they were nothing!" Ozzy shouts.

Patty goes over to Ozzy, visibly upset now. Ozzy stands face to face with her, tears and rage washed over his face.

"It's okay baby… We're not gonna let them get away," Patty consoles Ozzy, placing her hand on his cheek.

Ozzy looks into Patty's eyes and places one of his hands on her lower back. "We can't let them get away. And after what they did to our people, they gotta pay."

Patty looks lovingly into his eyes and speaks softly with a reassuring tone. "They're going to *beg* for death when we *do* get them too."

Ozzy pulls her in close and hugs her. One of the other men walks out of the gas station. "Oz, you might wanna come see."

18

◇

Everyone walks to the gas station and steps through the door with the broken glass, one by one. Ozzy walks over by the counter when he sees Jimbo's body and his head spread across the floor. "Fucking Christ. They got Jimbo too… FUCK!" Ozzy pushes over a shelving rack and all of the snacks, and foods spill onto the floor and the shelves break as it falls over. He kicks over a shelf with 2-liter sodas and slings a wire display rack with an assortment of trucker hats on it across the store as he storms out of the gas station, and everyone follows. This small mob now walks intently across the lot and into the road with a singular purpose.

"Ozzy, your gun," Virgil says, as he holds it out for Ozzy to take.

Ozzy takes the gun from him and tucks it in the back of his waistband. "Thanks."

"We follow where the car went into the field, find the car and we go from there. Keep quiet. No chit chat. We use hand signals. We don't wanna spook 'em. Not a lot of places to hide.

Listen to their movement. If they're in the fields, we'll hear them," Ozzy tells his devoted family as they cross the road.

The group all fall into a makeshift line as they come close to the spot where the car went off the road. Stalks of corn and sunflowers are snapped and scattered and it smells like burnt rubber and hot pavement. Kenny and Jasper enter into the thrashed foliage and everyone follows behind them, walking lightly so as to not make a ton of noise. Kenny walks ahead with a machete out and Jasper follows, just a few steps behind him with his hatchet at his side. Ozzy, Patty, Virgil and another man follow slowly on high alert. Kenny sees the car and all of the doors open, but no one is there. Kenny raises a fist to signal those behind him to stop. He looks around and they all listen and hear nothing. Jasper sees some broken stalks in an area where the car had not gone through. He looks back to everyone with two fingers pointing to his eyes then points to the suspicious spot as he takes the lead toward it.

Jasper steps into the matted down brush and broken stalks and they all maneuver through until they reach a dirt path clearing. They have run out of obvious places to track Olivia and Mike now and have to decide to go left or right. Kenny and Jasper turn to Ozzy.

"We goin' left or right?" Kenny asks.

Ozzy looks around for a moment. "We go left. There's no way they head back toward the road."

Jasper and Kenny go left and walk carefully as they survey for anything suspicious. As they approach the intersecting path, a man comes running, almost stumbling from the left as he turns right. It's Tom, who looks out of breath and is completely terrified. Tom bumps into Kenny and falls. Kenny has his knife ready and Jasper is right there ready to go. Tom looks up and sees that there is a gang of people with weapons looking for the people from the car. He is on his ass and kicks his feet against the dirt, backing away on the ground as he looks at everyone, stricken with fear.

"Who are you? Wh-what do you want?" Tom asks, panicked.

Jasper looks calmly to Tom and crouches down. "That uhh… that your car back there?"

Tom shakes struggling to answer. "That car, it's uh, what car?"

Jasper and Kenny look at each other. "So it is your car then?" Kenny asks.

Tom springs up to his feet and runs away and is stumbling around, not really running straight, or particularly fast. Tom has been running for a while. He is filthy and sweating profusely.

"Help! Somebody help!" Tom screams as he is running.

Tom hears someone running behind him and turns around to see Kenny coming at him in a full sprint. Tom's eyes open wider as he looks forward and continues to scream. "No! No! Leave me alone! Leave me alone!" Tom begs through his exhaustion. Kenny catches up to him and tackles him from behind and the two fall to the ground. Kenny wrestles Tom onto his back and mounts him like a cage fighter. Tom continues begging and pleading during the fading struggle, and Kenny holds a knife to his neck and waits for the rest of the group to get to them.

"Shhhh sh-sh-sh *relax*," Kenny says to Tom in a soothing tone.

Tom stares into his eyes and then down at his hand where he is holding the knife and just breathes quickly while he is in a subdued panic. The rest walk up and crowd around Tom.

"Get him up. On his feet," Ozzy orders Kenny.

Kenny pulls the knife away and grabs the front of his shirt and pulls him up. Ozzy speaks assertively to Tom. "Listen son, I'm only going to ask you this one time before your night gets really fuckin' bad." Tom stands there shaking and scared. "Where are your friends?"

Tom stares at him conflicted. "Who?"

Ozzy slaps Tom across the face, not too hard, but hard enough to get his attention and then grabbing his chin to force him to look at him. "You better understand the situation, real clear, boy. The guy and the girl. The ones you helped on the road." Patty steps into Tom's view and he recognizes her immediately. "We know you tried to help them. We know that's your car back there. It is in your best interest to tell me where they went."

Tom, terrified, and outnumbered, sees that these people are very serious. Tom stands there submissively, regretting not turning around. Moreso, he regrets even stopping at all. Olivia and Mike urged him in the car to go the other way and he insisted on not turning around, despite their warnings. Now he finds himself in this very bad position. He doesn't actually know where they are and he is afraid that if he doesn't give them something that they will kill him. He also knows if he lies they are even more likely to kill him. In an impulsive reaction, Tom jerks away from Kenny, breaking away into the clearing, and taking off again. Jasper gives chase and as he gets close enough he takes a swing with the hatchet and hits Tom's right shoulder blade. Tom lets out an agonizing scream and falls to the ground, writhing in pain.

Jasper grabs his right arm and slams it onto the ground, pinning it down by putting his boot onto Tom's wrist as he squirms. "STOP. MOVING!" Jasper barks.

Ozzy walks up to him and rolls his eyes. "Where are your friends? If you try bullshitting us, my brother Jasper here is gonna take that hatchet and take off your hand and probably make Thanksgiving turkey drawings later, long after you've rolled around here bleeding to death. Is that what you want? Sounds like a shitty way to spend your night, don't you think?"

Tom quickly shakes his head no. His face is white like a ghost and he is in pain from the wound on his back. "I don't know where they are–" Jasper puts his weight into standing on Tom's wrist. "Ahhhhhhhh! Please… Stop! I don't know where- I don't know where they are. The car- The car spun out and they were still trying to move, I-I got out and I took off. I don't know where they went. I- I really don't. Please!"

Everyone is staring at Ozzy waiting to see what he is going to say or do. Ozzy lets out a sigh. "Well that's not the least bit helpful now is it?" Ozzy draws the glock like a quickdraw cowboy and shoots Tom in the chest twice at close range. The shots ring out and Jasper lets his boot off of his arm. Tom lies on the ground staring at the stars as he bleeds out.

Jasper and Kenny grab his arms and legs and start to move him. "Leave him. Let the coyotes eat. We can come back for the bones," Ozzy says to them. They drop him onto the ground and the group continues onward through the clearing. They walk for a little bit through this field and are looking ahead into the darkness. Jasper and Kenny, leading the way still when they see they are coming to the end of this field. Kenny puts his fist up and everyone stops. He notices some lights turned on suddenly, off in the distance.

Kenny whispers to Jasper, "Those floodlights?"

Jasper looks back to Ozzy. "We gonna keep going?"

"Oh, I think we got 'em now," Ozzy says, with a smirk. They begin to walk out of the crops and into the yard.

"Looks like someone's house. Anyone we know?" Patty asks.

Ozzy stares, trying to focus through the light while holding his forearm over his eyes like a sun visor. "I don't know. Can't tell really… Shit, those lights are bright. Let's get closer."

The group takes steps toward the lights and as they're walking they hear a dog barking. Everyone stops and listens. They wait, quietly, under a tree, just listening. The dog's bark subsides after a few minutes and they hear voices but they're still too far away to make out what they're saying. After a minute or so, the talking stops entirely. Jasper looks to Ozzy, and Ozzy gives the nod to move forward. As they approach, they can see this is a large farmhouse with a lot of land. They continue a little more and they see a golden retriever standing at the base of the steps that lead up to the porch, and he sees them to and is barking at them.

Jasper and Kenny stop and are crouched with their weapons out. "What are we doing?" Jasper asks.

"We need to shut that dog up," Patty insists.

Jasper looks at Kenny. "Look man, I can't hurt a dog. You're gonna have to do this one."

Kenny looks offended. "Why the hell do I have to do it?" he asks.

"I can't man. I just can't, okay?" Jasper responds with conviction.

Virgil whispers loudly to Jasper and Kenny, "Maybe he's a friendly dog with a big bark and we can lure him over here. We can make it quick or something."

"How is that any better?" Kenny asks in a loud whisper.

"I can't kill man's best friend. This is where I draw the line," Jasper says firmly, crossing his arms, as if to put an exclamation mark on the statement.

Kenny pauses and stares at Jasper for a minute and snickers.

"What's funny?" Jasper asks.

"I just watched you drive a hatchet into a man's back and pin him to the ground while another man shot him in the chest… killing him. We're literally hunting down two human beings… and you won't kill… a dog," Kenny chirped.

Everyone in the group gives a quiet laugh, except Patty. "Well someone is going to need to go and cut the phone line. Just in case those two are inside, we need to make sure they can't call out for the police. Think of the dog as collateral damage," Patty suggests.

"I guess I'll do it then," Virgil says. He walks to the front, past Kenny and Jasper. "You guys are such sissies, lemme tell ya," Virgil says as he walks between them.

They watch Virgil walk toward the house and they wait, under the disguise of a big tree. The dog sees Virgil coming and he runs toward him. Virgil stops and the dog keeps a safe distance and continues to bark. He walks to the house and is very mindful of where the lights shine and where the shadows are. Walking around the carport, he sees a path to the side of the house. The dog follows him, still barking when Virgil clicks his tongue against the roof of his mouth to get a dog's attention. The dog becomes friendly and comes to Virgil with no fuss at all. Virgil pets him and his tail wags while his tongue hangs out of his mouth. Virgil looks at the dog and admires his well-groomed mane.

"You're a happy boy, huh? Aren't you?" Virgil says to the dog as he scratches his neck and around his ears. The dog licks Virgil's face and then lays on the ground. Virgil gets up and walks toward the house and the dog starts barking again. Virgil is out in the open, near the side of the porch. He looks at the dog and holds his finger to his mouth. "Shhhhhhhh!"

The dog happily wags his tail, barking, like he wants to play with his newfound backyard buddy. Virgil gets on one knee and calls the dog over to him. The dog comes to him as happy as a dog can be, with his tail wagging, tongue hanging out, and tags clanging off the metal piece of his collar whenever he moves. He nestles into Virgil's arms. Virgil pets him for a moment. "I'm sorry little buddy," he says to the dog, just before he puts him in a chokehold and slams him onto the ground in a headlock, squeezing as hard as he can, as he jerks his shoulder off of the ground, making the dog's neck pop. The dog's resistance stops instantly, and Virgil gets off of the ground, dusts himself off, and goes about his objective, to find the phone line and cut it off. He leaves the dog lying there in the yard.

19

◇

Before Ozzy's group arrived at the farmhouse…

Mike stands outside of the carport with his hands up, as the man on the porch points a rifle at him. "What are you doing out here?" the man asks, standing atop the steps, wearing blue jeans tucked into scuffed-up brown boots with a plain white shirt underneath an unbuttoned plaid shirt with the sleeves rolled up. He looks like he's in his late thirties, dark hair, kind of beady eyes, kind of tall, active-looking guy.

Before Mike can answer, the dog is rushing straight at him as fast as he can. Mike tenses up, expecting the dog to jump on him and attack. The dog slides in the dirt trying to stop, and he barks at Mike. He shakes off when he gets up and dirt poofs from his coat. He is very friendly and begins to sniff Mike. After he sniffs Mike, he sees Olivia hiding still and he is sniffing her. Olivia comes out of the carport next and shows her hands. The dog lowers the front of his body with his butt in the air and his tail wagging and he barks. He wants to play with his new friends.

Mike takes a step forward. "We're sorry. We just–"

"That's far enough, state your business. Why are the two of you in my backyard sneakin' round'?" the man asks with a firm hand on the rifle.

Mike steps back two steps. "Sorry… We're running. We were looking for a place to hide."

"Y'all do somethin'? Cops lookin' for yas?" the man asks quickly.

Mike snickers. "I would love to see a cop right now. We were hoping we could use your phone possibly. There are people that were after us. We were in an accident and they chased us," Mike explains to the man, as he stands awkwardly, squinting in the bright lights with his hands up.

"And you ran… Here?" the man asks, with implied suspicion in his tone.

Olivia steps beside Mike, looking up at the man, with her hand over her forehead to block the light. "We ran through that field trying to get as far from the road as possible and ended up here."

The man with the rifle stands poised and ready to shoot. He takes a good look at Mike and Olivia as they stand there looking up at him. "Seems like my dog likes you two… What's your names?"

"My name is Mike… This is Olivia," Mike answers.

"You're covered in blood Mike. You hurt?" the man on the porch asks.

Mike gestures one of his hands around his whole body where all of the blood is on his clothes. "All of this… Isn't as bad as it looks. I got knocked in my head a few times pretty good though."

The man points to Olivia with his gun, with one hand, like it's a pointing stick. 'And what about you dear? You hurt?"

"Just some bruises. I'm mostly just tired and looking for somewhere safe. I feel like I've been running all night," Olivia says to the man.

The voice of a woman calls out from inside the house, "Ben. What's going on out there?" As she is asking, she walks out onto the back porch. The woman looks like she is in her mid-thirties. She's wearing black tights and an oversized, plain t-shirt with a front pocket on it. She has dark hair and big beautiful eyes and an overall chipper way about her. "Oh– Hi there," she says to Mike and Olivia, with a look of confusion. She looks at Ben. "Babe, who are these people?"

Ben lowers the rifle and turns to the woman. "Well dear, this here is Mike, and that's Olivia," he says, pointing to each of them. "They're in trouble, they say and were in an accident." Ben turns to Mike and Olivia, "You guys, my name is Ben, this here is my wife, Cassie. And that guy down there, waiting for you to scratch his ears, that is Twinkie."

Olivia puts her hands down. "Could we please just use your phone for a second?"

Cassie looks at Ben for a moment. The couple have what appears to be an entire conversation without words, as their facial expressions go from wide grins, to wide eyes. Cassie turns to them, "Y'all come on inside. Let's get you cleaned up." Cassie opens the door and gestures for them to come in.

"Thank you so much!" Olivia says as she starts to come up the steps.

"We really appreciate this. Thank you. I know it's late. We're sorry," Mike says as he follows behind Olivia.

"It's alright. Come on inside. We will get you squared away. Cassie's a nurse and she's gonna get you fixed up," Ben says as Mike and Olivia walk past him.

They walk into the house and Ben and Olivia come in behind them. Cassie shuts the door, leaving Twinkie outside. The hallway leads into the kitchen, which is open and spacious. There are stairs to the right, inside the kitchen, leading upstairs, which has beautiful wood work on the banister and the spindles. There are wooden floors all throughout. The living room is through the kitchen ahead in the front of the house. The bathroom is to the left, directly off the kitchen. There is also a laundry room next to the bathroom. The kitchen has a common dinner table with six chairs around it, a kitchen island with a sink, and a baker's rack hanging above the island, loaded with pots and pans and some utensils. There is plenty of countertop and cabinetry space along the walls.

Cassie walks past them in the hallway. "Come on you two. We'll set up in the kitchen. Hon, will you go get me my first aid kit?"

Ben looks at Cassie, leans in and whispers to her, "You sure, you're okay with these two?"

"I'm fine. It'll take you two seconds. I'll holler if I need you," Cassie assures him.

Ben looks at her, and then at Mike and Olivia. "Alright. Be right back."

"Mike. You sit down there," Cassie says as she goes to the freezer with a sandwich bag. She puts ice in it and walks back over to Mike while she is zipping it up. "Put this on that knot on your head," she says to Mike as she hands him the ice pack. Cassie goes over to Olivia. "Honey, sink is right there, and the bathroom is through there," Cassie gestures to the sink and a doorway. "Go get yourself cleaned up a little."

"Thanks… Um… Where is your phone at?" Olivia asks, as she stands outside the bathroom.

"Phone is in the kitchen, on the counter, next to the coffee pot," Cassie says.

Olivia goes into the bathroom, shutting the door behind her, and leans her back against the door as she catches her breath. She puts her hand on her chest to feel her heart pounding still, closing her eyes and trying to take a deep breath as she focuses on what's happening around her, outside of the bathroom. The dog begins to bark again outside. Ben and Cassie can be heard talking to Mike but she can't make out what they're saying, just the sound of their voices. Olivia opens her eyes and exhales long and slow, looking at herself in the mirror in the small bathroom. She is lathered in dirt, grime, and dry blood. She uses the toilet then goes to the sink to wash her hands. The filth runs off of her hands and into the drain. Once her hands are clean, she shapes her hands like a bowl and splashes her face. She massages her face and continues to put water on it, grabs the hand towel, and wipes her face off as the towel comes away filthy.

Olivia comes out of the bathroom and sees Cassie in a chair sitting across from Mike, pouring rubbing alcohol onto a cotton swab. Ben is leaning against the kitchen counter. "I'm sorry. I used your hand towel and it's pretty dirty now."

"Don't sweat it," Ben says. He walks over and takes it from her and takes it to another room.

Cassie is cleaning up Mike's head when she notices the bruising on his jaw from the punch he took earlier in the evening from Cliff. She is moving his head around and looking and sees swelling on the back of his head from where Virgil hit him with the tow chain. She sees all of the dried blood on his hands and forearms. His clothing completely soiled from how his night has gone so far. Blood, sweat, dirt, and overall grime are the costume Mike wears at first glance.

"What's the story with all the blood?" Cassie asks as she is cleaning up his face.

Mike stares at her and hesitates, unsure how much to really say, considering the fact he murdered two men not too long ago. "We were attacked by some folks nearby. I was defending myself. I tried to save our friends."

"Where are your friends now?" Cassie asks.

Mike looks over to Olivia, and then back to Cassie. "They weren't so lucky, I wasn't able to save them."

Ben comes back into the kitchen. "What exactly happened out there?"

"There were four of us. We were on the road, and there was this group of older people. They had a church or cult or something in a big barn... Behind a gas station. Really strange... They held us captive and–" Olivia pauses as she looks over at Mike. She takes a breath. "Well they killed one of our friends."

"Wait... They actually *KILLED* someone?" Ben asks in disbelief.

"Well, what are we sitting around here talking for? The phone is right there," Cassie says, very animated as she points to the cordless phone on the kitchen countertop.

"There were two of our friends who were killed." Mike adds.

"And you mentioned out there that these people were chasing you?" Ben asks with a very serious demeanor. "Did they see you come here you think?"

Cassie begins to pack up her first aid kit. "I got you cleaned up as much as I can from here. You're gonna need a doctor to get that head looked at. You might have a concussion." Cassie opens up a drawer next to the sink and pulls out a bottle of Tylenol and tosses the bottle to Mike. "Here. Take those with you. I'm bettin' you're gonna have a nasty headache tomorrow, if you don't already."

Mike looks at the bottle. "Thanks."

"Of course!" Cassie says. "Why don't you go to the bathroom and wash your hands and get cleaned up a little. Maybe Ben can give you an old shirt so you don't have to wear that. Mike walks into the bathroom.

"Cassie. Call Twink in the house. We should lock up until the police get here," Ben says to Cassie as he begins to check his rifle, to make sure he is loaded. He is moving about a lot more quickly now, clearly on edge after hearing all of that.

Cassie walks out through the back door and onto the porch and calls for the dog. "Twinkie! Here boy!" There is no response. Cassie listens for his collar to jingle but doesn't hear anything. "That's weird. He usually comes runnin'." She steps out onto the porch to the top step and is looking out and calls again. "TWINKIE!"

Olivia stands at the counter and reaches for the phone. She picks it up from the base and turns it on, holds it to her ear and checks for the dial tone. So far, so good! She begins to dial 9-1-1 and as she puts the phone to her ear there is nothing. Olivia pulls the phone away from her ear and looks at it and the orange LED screen says "Dialing 911…" and the little dots are moving on the screen like it is waiting to connect. She puts it back to her ear and still nothing. She turns the phone off and back on and puts it to her ear and this time there is no dial tone. "No, no, no, no, no!" Olivia begins to panic all over again.

Ben looks over to her with concern. "What is it? What's the matter?"

"The phone. The phone! They cut the phone!" Olivia cries.

Ben walks over and takes the phone from her and sees on the screen "Dialing 911…" and he puts it to his ear and there is just silence. He presses the volume button and it is already at max volume. "Cassie…" he says out loud to himself. "CASSIE!" he yells as he jogs over to the back door. He sees Cassie standing there through the storm door at the top step.

Cassie stands at the top step after yelling for Twinkie and she looks around the backyard when the motion detecting flood lights turn off. This means that there has been no movement for at least two minutes if they turned off on their own. She is looking out into the deep, dark part of the yard, unable to really see anything now. "TWINKIE! COME HERE BOY! TREATS! I GOT TREATS!" Cassie yells.

Ben comes outside and stands beside Cassie. "He run off again?"

Cassie stands there with her arms crossed. "He always comes running. Especially when I say the T word."

"The phone isn't working. We should go inside, " Ben says to Cassie.

Ben walks back into the house and as Cassie is about to turn around to go in behind him, the motion sensor flood lights turn on again. Cassie walks back to the edge of the porch, at the top steps and she looks over to her right, near the side of the house when she sees Twinkie laying in the grass. Ben rushes back out onto the porch though when he hears Cassie scream. "No! Twinkie!" Cassie races down the stairs and into the yard.

20

◇

"Cassie! Wait!" Ben shouts. Cassie has already darted down the stairs and into the yard to check on the dog. "God dammit!" Ben mutters to himself as he goes back into the house and goes right for his rifle.

"What's going on?" Olivia asks, on high alert.

"Stay inside," Ben replies. Ben storms out the back door with the rifle in hand.

Olivia immediately starts tearing through drawers, looking for something to protect herself. She finds kitchen utensils, small cutlery, and dinnerware and then turns to the kitchen island and sees the baker's rack that hangs above it. She sees a stainless steel meat tenderizer hanging and she climbs onto the island and pulls it down. "MIKE! Come out here. We might have a problem!" Olivia shouts toward the bathroom.

As Ben comes out onto the porch, he sees Cassie down in the yard crying, and holding Twinkie. He begins to walk down the steps when a man appears from the side of the house. Cassies sees this man first and she stands up, with tears on her face and ferocity in her voice. "What the hell are you doing here? Did you kill my fucking dog?" She walks toward Virgil as he is coming from the side of the house.

Ben calls out to Cassie. "Honey. Come up here. NOW!" Ben points the gun at Virgil as he stands there frozen with his hands up. "We don't want no trouble. But I will one hundred percent shoot you dead right here if you don't get the fuck out of here right now. Cops are already on the way."

From the other side of the yard they hear a voice call out. "Did I hear somebody has treats?" Ozzy steps out of the shadows and into the light. Cassie turns to Ozzy, as Kenny, Jasper, and Patty are at his side, with weapons in their hands. Ben points the business end of the rifle at Ozzy.

"Stop right there!" Ben shouts out.

Ozzy stops and he shows his hands. "Whoa there. Eeeeasy John Wayne."

Everyone is looking up at Ben as he grips the gun, standing still as a rock, with full attention on Ozzy and his group.

"Get the fuck out of here!" Cassie charges over to Ozzy with urgency in her legs and pain on her face. "Who do you think you are? You just walk into our yard and kill our fucking dog! What do you want?" Cassie gets in his face and shoves him hard enough to make him stumble back a bit.

Ozzy catches his balance. "Hey now! Let's just calm d–"

"What kind of person does that?" Cassie screams as she pushes him once more.

"CASSIE!" Ben yells.

Ozzy backs up a little more and begins to chuckle a little bit. "I'll give you that. You're clearly upset. I get it. But you–" SMACK! Cassie smacks Ozzy across the face.

Ben comes running down the stairs in an onset of panic. "CASSIE! STOP!" Virgil walks over near the stairs as Ben sees him coming. Ben points the gun at Virgil. "Back off!" Virgil slows down to a stop. Ben walks cautiously down to the yard with his finger on the trigger, as he eyeballs Ozzy and Virgil. "Cassie. Baby. Please, just get in the house," Ben says calmly.

Olivia walks over to the storm door and peeks outside and can barely see what's going on but she can hear the commotion outside. She hears Ben and Cassie yelling at someone. Mike comes out of the bathroom and he goes upstairs while Olivia stands by the door.

Cassie turns her back to Ozzy, and looks at Ben, broken.

"I think you might have a couple friends of ours in your house. *Bee-E-Ay-utiful* house by the way… And look, guys, I'm sorry about the dog. Truly. But if you're hiding someone from us, this might not end well for you two. You're gonna wanna hand over those two kids you got in there." Ozzy says to Ben and Cassie. "They've done awful things. Even killed a few of our friends. And when the cops come, you don't wanna be an accomplice do you?"

"Cassie. Come on," Ben says to her nervously.

As she takes a step toward Ben, turning her back to Ozzy and his people, Patty quickly glides past Jasper, and past Ozzy with the jungle knife in her hand. Ben sees Patty moving but Cassie is in his shot. Patty walks up behind Cassie and before she could turn around to react, Patty pulls her hand back and with great force shoves it into Cassie's lower back with a roaring yell.

Cassie tenses up from the sharp point of the blade tearing through her back and slicing through her vital organs. Her face is full of horror.

"NOOOO!" Ben screams. As he puts his finger on the trigger, Virgil rushes him and knocks the gun to face the ground as Ben fires a shot into the grass. Everyone jumps as the shot's bang growls into the quiet night. Ben pulls the gun back up and he takes the stock of the rifle and tries to hit Virgil. Virgil grabs the rifle's barrel with one hand and the stock of the gun with the other hand as Ben fights and pushes against Virgil. Ben pushes Virgil back and overpowers him entirely, Virgil lands on his back and Ben climbs on top of him and presses the rifle into his throat.

Patty continues to shove the knife into Cassie's back, all the way to the hilt. Cassie tries to speak, but is focused on what just happened, looking down slowly as she sees the tip of the knife poking out of her stomach with blood draping over the knife and spilling down the front of her stomach.

"I'm not sorry honey. You don't get to put your hands on my husband like that," Patty hisses before abruptly pulling the knife out of her back and pushing her forward, to fall flat on her face. Patty then steps back to stand at Ozzy's side as she wipes the blood off of the knife against her pants. Cassie lies on the ground, face down, attempting to crawl, but unable to use her strength to get up. She lies there and her head falls and she can see Ben on top of Virgil.

Ben continues to press as hard as he can into Virgil's throat and is so blind with fury that he is completely detached from the situation around him. As Ben is screaming in a fit of rage, Virgil is struggling to breathe or fight Ben off. Virgil looks up to see Ben screaming with wild eyes and clenched teeth as he breathes and spits uncontrollably. Kenny comes up behind Ben and grabs his hair and jerks his head back. Before Ben can even steady himself to fight, Kenny takes his knife and slices his throat in one swift motion. The blood sprays out immediately after and Kenny holds onto Ben's head for a few seconds to really let the blood gush. The blood rushes down the front of Ben's shirt and gets all over Virgil, who tosses the gun away as he catches his breath and he crawls backwards, away from Ben.

Patty comes over and grabs the rifle from the ground. She checks to see if there are bullets in it and loads the chamber. She puts the gun under her arm as she proceeds to wipe off the knife.

"Did you… Have to… Do that… Right on me? You dick!" Virgil asks Kenny as he tries to regulate his breathing.

Kenny laughs so hard that he can barely speak. "You should have seen your face brother." Kenny lets go of Ben and lets him fall to the ground. Ben slams onto the ground and he is facing Cassie. His eyes widen as he tries to speak, but he is choking on his own blood, as he lies there with his hands on his throat, desperately trying to stop the bleeding. Cassie moves slightly but is too weak, and unable to do much of anything now. She looks at Ben dying as she tries to speak but she only coughs up blood, in great pain with each violent cough, as she lies in a pool of her own blood. Ben and Cassie bleed to death looking into each other's eyes.

21

◇

Olivia backs away from the storm door, slams the main door shut and locks it. She locks the handle lock, the deadbolt, and even the little chain. She backs away, looking at the door, with a meat tenderizer in her right hand. "Mike?" Olivia calls out. She looks around the kitchen trying her best to not panic. This night, so far, only seems to offer running or hiding as ways to pass the time.

Mike is upstairs in the office digging through the drawers of a filing cabinet. "Yeah?" he hollers.

Olivia walks over to the base of the steps. "We need to get out of here. They're here," she yells up the stairs. "I think something bad just happened outside!"

Mike slams the drawer shut. "Shit," he says under his breath, as he looks around the room. He sees an autographed Louisville Slugger baseball bat mounted on the wall in the office. There is an engraved plate underneath it that reads 'Ronald Acúna Jr. 2020 National League Silver Slugger,' The wall in this office is curated with all sorts of sports memorabilia. Mike rips the bat off of the wall, gripping the handle of it while admiring the barrel and hardly legible signature. He shrugs and rests it over his right shoulder as he makes his way to the stairs, rushing down the steps to join Olivia in the hallway, as she is focused on the back door. She looks at Mike as he gets into a batter's stance.

"Nice," she says.

"Is that a meat tenderizer?" Mike asks.

"Yeah" she replies, without taking her eyes off the back door.

"Do you think we should try to make a break for it out the front door?" Mike asks.

Olivia turns and looks into the living room and back to the back door. "What if they're out there? They're probably surrounding the place!"

"We can fight our way out," Mike suggests quickly.

"How many do you think are out there?"

"I don't know. They could have their entire group looking for us right now."

A shadow appears through the curtain that covers the back window. They can see two silhouettes outside. Someone begins to turn the door knob, and it bangs against the door frame as someone is slamming their body into the door. They back up and kick the door several times in succession but it doesn't budge. Mike and Olivia stand ready to attack. The shadows disappear for a moment as Olivia keeps her eyes on the door. The tension is high as Mike and Olivia anticipate what might come next. As they watch the door anxiously, a shadow appears, and comes close to the door. The person punches the glass multiple times and the sound of their fist hitting sends echoes through the house with each hit causing Mike and Olivia to flinch with each hit.

Eventually, one of the glass panes breaks and an arm reaches through, wrapped in a dirty t-shirt. The hand shakes and the shirt unravels and drops to the floor. Mike comes toward the door and swings the bat and hits the arm as they unlock the door knob. The person pulls the arm out quickly.

"Stay the fuck out! I'll knock your fucking head off motherfucker!" Mike shouts at the door. Mike waits, cocked and ready for gametime. "Stay back Liv!" There is a kick at the door, this time busting the frame on the inside a bit as the glass from the broken window rattles along with the impact of the kick. "No!" Mike says as he sees the door frame separating from the interior wall.

BAM! Another kick does major damage to the door. Mike backs up a little, realizing he cannot keep them from kicking the door down at this point. Another kick sends the entire door and frame crashing onto the hallway floor. Kenny stands there with no shirt on, holding his forearm against his body, bleeding from the glass. Patty steps in, and walks on top of the toppled door and into the hallway and she raises the rifle. Patty backs Mike up at gunpoint and as she steps into the open part of the kitchen. Olivia rushes Patty, tackling her into the wall, jarring her so hard she drops the rifle onto the floor.

"You hit pretty hard, for a little baby!" Patty mutters as she tries to get back to her feet.

Kenny sees Mike distracted and lunges at him. Mike reacts quickly enough and hits Kenny in the shoulder with the bat. Kenny winces as he absorbs the hit. He reaches for Mike and as Mike takes a second swing, Kenny grabs the barrel of the bat mid-swing, and twists Mike's wrist backwards, causing him to let it go. Mike spins his way out of the hold and gets into a lower position to scoop Kenny up and slam him into the kitchen floor really hard. This knocks the wind out of Kenny.

Olivia is on her feet and Patty is on one knee, rising to her feet as Olivia raises the meat tenderizer over her head. As she goes to swing it, Ozzy comes in and grabs her forearm and slams her hand back into the hallway wall. She drops the meat tenderizer onto the floor and it lands with a heavy thud, and bounces away. Patty then seizes the opening and rushes Olivia at close range and drives her shoulder into Olivia's stomach, slamming her against the wall.

Mike hops on top of Kenny and grabs both sides of his head, covering his ears, and pulls it up away from the floor and slams it back as hard as he can. Mike is growling as he displays his power and his wrestling ability. He slams Kenny's head into the floor several more times. Ozzy sees Mike on top of Kenny with the advantage and he draws the glock. Ozzy walks over and fires a shot as he raises it. The bullet misses Mike and hits a cabinet door. Mike tenses up at the shot. He stands up and rushes at Ozzy, going low, and he smacks his arm away. Ozzy lets off another shot as his arm is knocked away. Mike wraps his arms around Ozzy and starts to lift him off the ground when Ozzy raises his arm driving his elbow into the top of Mike's back. He delivers another blow as Mike releases the grip and backs away.

Patty stands up after she tackles Olivia. Olivia grabs her head in pain after it bounces off the wall. Patty then grabs Olivia's hair, jerks her head really hard to the side, and uses her body to drive her shoulder into Olivia. Olivia is pinned between Patty and the wall as Patty grabs a handful of her hair and drives her shoulder against her once more. Patty reaches her other hand back and punches Olivia in the face. Olivia shrieks in pain after the punch. Patty releases her hair and grabs the right shoulder strap of Olivia's tank top and she slings her into the wall across the hallway. Olivia bounces off the wall and sees Patty coming at her quickly. Olivia turns to her side and as Patty gets closer she fires an elbow into Patty's face. Patty is stunned and staggers.

Patty holds her mouth and grins and two of her front teeth are broken. "You little bitch!"

Olivia lets out a scream, and with all of her energy, all of her rage, she charges at Patty, shoving her with her forearms out in front like she is blocking in football. Patty stumbles backwards and trips over the door lying on the floor. Patty falls onto what is left of the exposed shards of glass and cuts up her hands on the landing.

Ozzy turns his attention away from Mike, over to Olivia who is standing over Patty on the ground, sitting bloody, practically stuck. Olivia stands there with her fists balled up staring daggers through Patty. Patty looks at her hands and then up at Olivia as her anger shoots right back at Olivia. Ozzy comes from behind and wraps both of his arms around Olivia. "I gotcha!" Ozzy says. Olivia kicks and fights to break free to no avail. Patty carefully tries to get to her feet, but is pulling glass out of her hands. Ozzy lifts Olivia off the ground when Olivia lets out a vicious grunt and slings her head backwards as hard as she can. She hits Ozzy in the face so hard that his grip loosens.

"OWWW! FUCKING CHRIST!" Ozzy yells, releasing Olivia and grabbing his nose. Olivia quickly turns and drives a herculean knee into Ozzy's groin. Ozzy's eyes close tightly and he lets out a wheezing, nasally breath. The look on his face as he crumbles to the floor, although not making an audible sound, speaks volumes of how bad that had to hurt.

As Mike stands there watching, Kenny has gotten up and attacks Mike from behind, putting him in a chokehold. Mike moves his body to try and get enough momentum to toss Kenny off of him but Kenny has a death grip and is applying pressure with all of his strength. "AAAAHHHHH!" Kenny belts as he squeezes and tries to pull back to hyperextend Mike's body.

After Ozzy hits the floor, Olivia looks around frantically. She sees the meat tenderizer on the floor and picks it up. She raises it above her head, while looking at Kenny. With a feral roar she hits Kenny in the back of the head with it. Kenny immediately lets go of Mike and he drops to his knees, staggering across the kitchen and catches himself on the kitchen island. He turns and rests his back against it to prevent falling and he reaches up to feel his head and he looks at his hand and he has fresh blood on all of his fingertips. "Ah fuck," Kenny says in disappointment, feeling the blood trickling down the back of his neck.

Olivia goes over to Kenny with the meat tenderizer in hand, visible blood on the textured side. With her hair a mess and wrath written on her face, she walks over and gets close to Kenny, he reaches back onto the baker's rack and tries to grab a skillet that hangs above him on the baker's rack. As he is reaching, Olivia whacks him across the face, smashing his cheek with the meat tenderizer. He slouches lower after the hit, completely stunned, and Olivia issues another crushing blow to his temple. He slumps further, hitting the floor as his legs give out. She swings another, hitting him in the mouth. Kenny lies there with his face reconfigured, and motionless after the fourth hit.

Olivia screams, swinging faster, but with shorter range, and lands six more shots to his mutilated face. His body falls all the way to the floor and his caved in face is making a bloody mess on the kitchen floor. His nose is folded over to the left side of his face. The blood spatters and sprays from Kenny's face during this vicious assault leaving Olivia standing there with her once light gray tank top, saturated in the dirt and grime from the evening, and the front of her body completely bloodsoaked.

Mike picks up the baseball bat. Patty has since gotten up and has picked up the rifle and is pointing it at Mike. "Drop it!"

Patty stands over Ozzy as he raises to his feet, holding onto his crotch, slow to get up. "Come on hun. Get up… Ya good?" Ozzy gets on both feet and sighs, nodding yes.

Olivia turns to them. Patty points the rifle at her, and she notices Kenny on the floor. "Oh no… Kenny," her voice cracks.

Ozzy looks over and sees Kenny. "Are you fucking serious? You little cunt! A meat tenderizer! Really?" He takes a couple steps toward Olivia and she takes a couple steps back as she holds up the meat tenderizer, like it's a knife. Ozzy is unbothered by her mannerisms and marches at her.

Patty has the rifle pointed toward Olivia, and Mike still has the bat in his hand. He takes the opening and lunges at Patty, knocking the rifle sideways with a backhanded swing of the slugger. As he does that, the barrel points to the ceiling and she fires a shot. The bang echoes through the house. Right at that moment, the living room door in the front is kicked in by Jasper and Virgil. Olivia looks over toward the living room as the two men come in and as soon as she does, Ozzy slaps her so hard that her entire body bangs against the kitchen island. She instinctively lashes out aimlessly with the meat tenderizer, missing wildly, and Ozzy thrusts a front kick into her chest, knocking her halfway across the kitchen. She drops the weapon and crashes to the floor.

Ozzy walks over with authority and he punches her in the face, knocking her back flat onto the floor. Everything is in slow motion as she opens her eyes just a few seconds after. Everything is unfolding so quickly now, but it feels like an eternity to her as she is nearly helpless to fight after taking the hits from Ozzy. She sees Mike knock Patty over in the hallway, and he takes off up the stairs in a hurry. Ozzy pulls the glock out and holds it in Olivia's face. Jasper and Virgil come storming through from the living room, pursuing Mike. They blaze up the stairs and Olivia is stunned. She closes her eyes and passes out.

22

◇

Ozzy puts the glock back into the front of his waistband as Olivia passes out. Patty follows Jasper and Virgil up the stairs in a hurry. Mike scrambles up the stairs and bursts into one of the bedrooms. He looks at the closet and considers hiding in there. *No, that's too obvious. Under the bed? That's even more obvious.* Mike looks at the window. He hears them racing upstairs like a thunderous stampede. Mike runs to the window and he opens the curtain to see that there is roof access. Without a second thought, he opens the window, hopping out onto the roof. The roof is slanted and is a lot more treacherous to maneuver, versus how it looks. Mike steps sideways as fast and careful as he can. He reaches an even steeper part of the roof that goes to the third floor. Virgil leans his head out to see Mike escaping.

"Hey! You're only makin' this harder on yourself boy!" Virgil yells out. Mike ignores him and begins to slowly climb up the steeper part of the roof.

Virgil pokes his head back inside. "That fucker is going even higher!" he says to Jasper.

"Well get out there!" Jasper orders.

Virgil looks at him, offended. "I can't get across that roof," he says as he puts his hands on his stomach and jiggles his belly.

"Get out of the way you fat fuck!" Jasper nudges Virgil aside and steps out with one leg.

"Hey! Why you gotta take it there brother?" Virgil snaps back.

"You just jiggled your own belly, should I comment on how old you are?" Jasper jabs.

"Well at least I ain't too soft to shut the dog up," Virgil said proudly.

Patty walks into the room. "Boys, boys! Knock it off. We gotta catch him."

Virgil shakes his head in disapproval. Jasper looks onto the roof, becoming hesitant to step out.

"What's wrong?" Patty asks.

Jasper looks at her with embarrassment. "I'm scared of heights. I can't do it."

"You're scared of heights?" Patty fires back.

"You dog lovin' son of a bitch!" Virgil barks.

"I don't know what to tell you! I'm scared of heights!" Jasper shouts.

Virgil chuckles while Jasper and Patty go back and forth. "You call me fat, but you're a chicken-shit when it comes to heights."

Patty pushes Jasper aside and leans out the window and looks around.

Mike has scaled the roof and hid himself alongside a brick chimney. He leans against it, with his feet at an awkward angle, unsure what he should do, or what he can do.

"Hey! What's going on up there?" Ozzy hollers up the stairs.

Jasper stares at Patty in silence, hesitating on what to say to Ozzy. Patty shouts back, "The boy escaped through the window. We can't get to him."

Ozzy is confused. "What do you mean, can't get to 'em?"

"He's on the roof and we don't see him now," Jasper shouts back.

Ozzy looks down at the floor and then over to Olivia as she lies there knocked out. "Alright. Come on down."

Patty exhales with an annoyed look on her face. "Come on," she says to the guys. Virgil shuts the window and locks it. The three head out of the bedroom and make their way down the stairs and meet with Ozzy in the kitchen.

"Alright, here's what we're gonna do. We're gonna take the girl. We keep her alive and use her for The Cleansing. We should get her back before the sun comes up," Ozzy advises, confidently.

Patty goes over to Olivia and kicks her foot to no reaction. "What's the plan with the girl? Somebody has to carry her."

Ozzy sighs. "Well… We carry her back, begin preparations for The Cleansing, hope the boy comes for her, and then we kill him."

"Ozzy, we can't just let him go. He's going to rat us out if he gets away!" Virgil prompts.

"Well, what do you propose?" Ozzy asks.

"Well, I guess I don't have any better suggestions," Virgil replies.

Ozzy walks over to the counter and sees the cordless phone. He checks the call history and sees the LED screen still says 'Dialing 9-1-1…' He ends the call and checks the history and there was no actual call that got through to emergency dispatch. He removes the battery and leaves it on the counter next to the phone.

Jasper crouches down close to Kenny's body. He hangs his head low and says a prayer to himself.

Virgil sees Kenny and he looks away. "What are we gonna do about Kenny, boss?"

Ozzy responds quickly. "Leave him. We'll send people in the morning to clean this up right."

"And the girl?" Patty asks.

"Virgil can carry her. We'll take turns if we need to," Ozzy replies quickly.

Virgil groans as he goes over to Olivia. He grabs her hand and pulls her up and he puts her in a fireman's carry position.

Ozzy walks out of the kitchen, into the hallway, and takes careful steps onto the backdoor that is lying unstable on the floor. The others follow behind him and they stop on the porch.

Ozzy looks down the stairs, into the yard and sees Ben, Cassie and the dog's bodies. "Jasper. Help me bring them into the house please. Gonna have a lot to do tomorrow."

Jasper sets his hatchet down and he makes his way down the stairs. "Let's get this done." Jasper walks over and grabs the dog first. He sees a tarp in the carport loosely hanging on a car and he pulls it off. He uses the tarp to wrap the dog up. He picks the dog up after he delicately wraps him in the tarp and he carries him up the steps, and into the house, laying him on the kitchen floor next to a food dish that is outside of the laundry room.

Jasper heads back outside as Ozzy and Patty are grabbing Ben by the hands and feet and carrying him over to the base of the stairs. Jasper comes down the steps and goes over to Cassie.

He reaches down and grabs her feet and drags her over and leaves her next to Ben.

"Ready?" Jasper asks Ozzy.

"Yeah," Ozzy groans, annoyed.

They both grab Ben and carry him up the stairs like an awkward piece of furniture, Ozzy walking backwards up the steps. They carry him in and leave him on the kitchen floor, right beside Kenny.

They walk out and down the stairs and repeat with Cassie's body. This time Jasper walks backwards up the stairs. Cassie is a little lighter than Ben so they are able to move a little faster this time. They carry her through the hallway and drop her in Ben's lap.

Ozzy slaps his hands together alternating up and down like he's dusting them off. "All done! Let's head back."

Jasper opens the refrigerator and grabs a bottle of beer. He closes the fridge and bangs the neck of the bottle against the counter, knocking the cap off perfectly. He takes a big swig and when he pulls it away from his mouth he wipes the foam off of his lips and lets out a nourished gasp and smiles.

Ozzy stares at him in awe.

"…What?" Jasper asks, with an uncomfortable look on his face.

"Just admiring the moment. We just made a pile of bodies, and you go for the fridge," Ozzy says to Jasper, with a grin.

Jasper puts his hands up, shrugging. "I was thirsty!" he says as he takes another drink. "Matter of fact," he opens the fridge again and grabs another beer and sticks it into his back pocket.

Ozzy shakes his head laughing as he watches Jasper. "Un-fucking-believable."

Jasper smiles and takes another drink as the two walk back outside and down the steps to meet with Patty and Virgil. Virgil has Olivia on the ground and has found some zip ties that were in a tool chest underneath the back porch, and he is securing Olivia's wrists as she is still unconscious. Patty is standing in a small flower bed admiring the various perennials in full bloom.

"Virgil. You carry her," Ozzy orders. "We can all take turns. Let's hope she doesn't wake up." Virgil huffs as he pulls her arms up from the ground and he hoists her up over his shoulder again, making several grunts in the process. As everyone puts their back to the farmhouse, Ozzy stops for a second and turns back. "Hold up a second," he calmly says to everyone. They all stop and Ozzy takes a couple steps toward the house. "I don't know if you're hiding somewhere but if you're hearing my voice, just know that your friend here, we're gonna take her back to the compound. We're going to split her open and show the world how nasty you people are on the inside. And make sure she's alive to feel as much of it as possible," Ozzy projects.

Ozzy pauses and listens closely. Meanwhile, Mike is still on the roof hiding alongside a chimney, out of sight, hearing everything Ozzy says.

"You can do yourself a favor. You can't save her… but you can guarantee we make it quick. Come on out. Make this easy, boy!" Ozzy pauses again. He looks back to Jasper, Patty, and Virgil. They just watch him. He turns back toward the house. "Well alright… You know where she will be then. The Cleansing begins soon… Hope to see ya there." Ozzy turns and the four walk off back to the compound the way they came, with Olivia on Virgil's back.

Mike waits, clenching the brick chimney, standing upright with his back against the bricks, trying not to make a sound. He watches clouds passing by the moon, unsure what his next move is. *Do I save myself and run out the front door and never look back? Or do I try to save Olivia before something terrible happens to her?*

23

Mike looks around after several minutes have passed and realizes that Ozzy and his people have taken Olivia away. He cranes his neck around the side of the chimney and looks out into the yard and doesn't see or hear anyone. He brings his head back slowly and takes a few deep breaths before he makes the climb back to the bedroom window. The roof is at an impractical incline for climbing. He is careful as he navigates his way back to the window with careful footing and coordination. When he gets back to the window he sees that it is closed.

He tries to open it but it is locked. "Fuck," he says under his breath, annoyed. He looks around and there really are no alternatives other than going through this window or dropping down into the yard, but he is unable to see what is below him from his vantage point. It is very dark and even if he somehow triggered the motion lights, it would not shine on this side of the house. Mike sits on the window sill and unties his shoe, pulls it off, and bangs on the glass with the heel of the shoe. The window is sturdy and not breaking, just making a lot of noise as he hits it. "Shit!" he says, bracing himself as he bangs his shoulder into the window at close range. The pane of glass seems more likely to push inward than it does breaking.

Another slam into the window and he sees the seals around the edges moving as he crashes into it. He uses his shoe again as a makeshift hammer, pounding along the edges of the window. After he bangs the shoe-hammer along all sides and throws his shoulder into the center of the glass once more, finally the glass comes apart from the frame. He sees the weak point and pushes against it until it comes off enough for him to reach his arm through and unlock it. He does this and pulls his arm back out and opens the window. Once he is inside he closes the window, and sits on the bed to collect himself.

As Mike lies down on the bed, he gets lost in his thoughts, thinking of times when he would hang out with Kris, Nathan, or Olivia, thinking of the conversations they would have, about all of the nuances in those individual relationships that will only be memories now. Kris and Nathan were victims to a sick band of psychopaths, but Olivia is still alive, as far as he knows. Ozzy's words replay in his head about torturing her unless he comes for her. He sits up in the bed and knows that he wouldn't be able to live with himself if he didn't at least try to help Olivia. Mike knows this is suicide and that he isn't the hero-type at all.

Mike begins to take a closer look around the bedroom. He looks under the bed, inside of the nightstands, the shelves inside the closet, and he doesn't find anything of use. *A simple fully loaded pistol would be nice to find.* He goes back into the office he was in earlier and begins to open all of the desk drawers and sees miscellaneous items and things you would expect to be in an office desk. He opens the closet door and there is a gun safe, but it takes a security pin. "Shit!" Mike says. He tugs on the handle, hoping maybe it wasn't closed all the way, but Ben seems to have been a responsible gun owner. It was locked safe and secure.

Mike goes into another bedroom that seems to be an unused guest room. The dresser in there is empty, nothing in the closet really, just a clean, well-kept bedroom. He heads back downstairs and sees Ben and Cassie's bodies next to Kenny. Kenny's face is grotesque and disfigured, sitting slumped over, on the floor against the kitchen island. Ben's throat is sliced wide open. Cassie's shirt and pants are completely blood-soaked. Mike stands at the bottom of the stairs and looks at them and loses his stomach onto the floor. He wipes his mouth and as he is gasping, walks over to the sink and spits into it. He opens a cabinet and grabs a glass and has a drink of water at the sink. He puts cold water on his face from the faucet, turns it off and goes back to looking around the house.

He goes into the living room and there is a large sectional couch and matching recliner, a bookshelf, and a large flat screen TV mounted on the wall above a fireplace. The front door is open from when it was kicked in earlier. There is a coffee table with some drawers in it. He checks the drawers and under the couch cushions, where he finds nothing of interest. He goes over to the fireplace and sees the fireplace poker and picks it up. He admires it closely and puts his index finger on the pointy end. "Hmmph, this will do I suppose," he says, resting it against his shoulder.

He walks out the front door and sees a big front yard, with a long gravel driveway, and a pickup truck and SUV parked close to the house. The front porch has a nice porch swing and beautiful flower beds along the porch. Mike turns back to go inside and heads into the kitchen with the fireplace poker in his hand. He looks at Ben and Cassie's bodies once more, this time not as disgusted, but just saddened. "I'm sorry," he says.

He walks out through the back door, onto the back porch and makes his way down the staircase. As he walks onto the stairs, the motion sensor lights come on. He stops and looks around for a moment to make sure someone is not waiting for him to come out, but is only greeted with silence.

He goes into the carport and is looking around and sees some miscellaneous things lying about. There is a skinny folding table with an assortment of car parts and greasy rags on it. There is an older metal toolbox that looks like it's banged around over the last handful of decades, paint scraped off mostly, and it makes a ton of noise as Mike opens it to look inside. There is a staple gun, screwdrivers, a hammer, pliers, some random screws and fasteners, a level, reading glasses, dirty leather gloves, and a tattered up, spiral notepad. Mike rummages through and finds a key in the mix. He sees a Plymouth logo on it and notices the car in the carport has the tarp removed now and that it is also a Plymouth.

He puts the key into the lock on the door and it works. He gets inside the car and looks around. It's clean and well-maintained. He opens the glove box and finds a first aid kit, a shop rag and some sunglasses. He closes the glove box and starts feeling around under the driver seat and he feels something hard. He pulls it forward and grabs it. He looks down and with a turn of luck it's a handgun. He holds it up into the light and it's a common, short barrel revolver. He opens the spindle and there are only two bullets in it. "Sweet!" he whispers to himself.

He steps out of the car and closes the door and leaves the key on the folding table. He walks out into the yard, heading toward the tall grass and crops that he and Olivia came through to get here earlier. With a pistol grip sticking out of his pocket and a fireplace poker resting over his shoulder, he begins his journey back to the compound, in hopes of saving his good friend Olivia.

24

◇

Virgil walks several paces behind Ozzy, Patty, and Jasper. "I'll catch up. Don't you worry about me," Virgil shouts, as he is practically dragging himself back to the compound, sweating and flat out exhausted. Ozzy and Patty walk ahead as they are eager to get back to the compound with Olivia captured. Jasper has her over his shoulder, still knocked out as he pushes onward right behind Ozzy and Patty, with his hatchet slid into the belt loop of his jeans, and the handle banging off his thigh as he takes each step.

"What's the plan when we get back brother?" Jasper asks.

Ozzy responds with his head forward, and eyes ahead. "Well, I imagine we get the girl cleaned up, get her situated, and we begin the process. I have that feeling that tonight is the night though." Patty looks over at Ozzy, as she paces alongside him, with a rifle in hand, and blood on her face. Ozzy shoots a look over to her with a smile. "I just have that feeling." They continue to walk through the smashed, and trampled stalks of corn and sunflowers in mostly silence. Ozzy then reaches for his walkie talkie.

"This is Big Brother, to Homebase. Anybody have a copy? Over."

Almost immediately, Ozzy responds. "Go for Homebase."

"We have precious cargo in tow. Might be a good idea to begin preparations for The Almighty's arrival. Over," Ozzy announces with a confidence radiating from him.

"Copy that, brother. See you soon. Over."

As their voyage on foot nears its end, Ozzy and Patty come out of the tall grass, and meet the road. Jasper and Virgil are not far behind. Two men run up to them who are patrolling the road and are relieved to see that it is Ozzy.

"You're gonna wanna stay out here a while longer. We may have company coming not far behind us. We have the girl, the boy is not important. Be ready to kill him… On sight," Ozzy orders.

"Of course, brother," one of the loyal soldiers says. The two of them turn back and walk along the road on lookout duty.

Patty and Jasper walk ahead, crossing the street while Ozzy talks to the men. One of the guys from the compound meets them in the lot, and takes Olivia off of Jasper's shoulder to relieve him. Jasper immediately rotates his shoulder to try and loosen things back up after the walk back that seemed like forever with a one-hundred-and-fifty-pound girl on his shoulder. Virgil comes out and is dragging behind them all as they head inside the compound.

As they all come inside, the church members are moving quickly inside in preparation for what comes next. People are pairing up to move the picnic tables and the chairs that are scattered throughout the floor. They are working to open up the common space. As Ozzy marches through, he is shaking hands and practically celebrating with a smile, like some kind of politician. Hugs and words of affirmation are spat at Ozzy and some even to Jasper, Patty, and Virgil.

"Where's Kenny?" one woman shouts from across the barn.

Patty hears it, and quickly looks at Ozzy, as if she doesn't know how Ozzy plans to tell people what happened. Ozzy stops and turns to the woman and his smile is overtaken with a look of distress. He walks over to her and lowers his head, and he looks up at her, somberly. Without saying anything the woman immediately breaks down and buries her face into his chest and wraps her arms around him. He puts his arms around her tight and holds her close. Her loud weeping and cries are muffled, lost in his chest.

"It's alright sister," he consoles her, rubbing his hand up and down her back and letting her have this moment to bear her heartbreak. "I know… I know…" The people around are working at a slower pace, while others completely stop altogether. Some begin to cry and console one another. There is a great sense of loss in the room and the enthusiasm has been sucked out now after people have put together that something happened to Kenny while they were out. Some are angry. Most are devastated at the amount of loss the community has suffered tonight.

The woman pulls away from Ozzy and wipes her eyes on the topside of her hands. "Did he suffer? Please tell me it was at least quick."

Ozzy places his hand on her shoulder and looks up at her and into her eyes, "It was quick." Patty makes eye contact with

Ozzy and says nothing because she knows it was not quick at all. This small lie helps ease the pain in the moment though.

The woman breaks down again into a flurry of tears. "Where is he?" she asks through a crumbling voice.

"I'll send a group out in the morning. He is somewhere safe though," Ozzy assures her.

As people are clearing the floor, one of the men secures a rope from one of the support rafters. As the rope is dangling near the center-most part of the barn, a woman begins drawing a circle on the floor around it with what looks like sidewalk chalk, and she adds symbols inside of it. The rope is secured and hanging about six feet off of the ground. Jasper and Virgil take Olivia over, cut the zip ties, and begin to tie her wrists together to string her up properly. Virgil raises her up to allow Jasper to be able to get her hands nice and tight.

"Hey. Go ahead and gimme a lil' slack for now brother," Jasper says to the guy who set up the rope. "We'll just leave her on the floor until she comes to, and then we can string her up."

The man unties the rope from the beam and Virgil sets her on the ground and they tie her up. Virgil looks at the man as he wipes sweat from his forehead. "Now, if you see her start to move around and get to wakin' up, you pull on that rope, stand her up. Can't be lettin' her get too much freedom now can we?"

"I got ya brother," says the rope handler.

Patty and Ozzy are off in a corner now, in the kitchen area. Ozzy is setting all of his things down. Patty is leaning against the wall. "Do you believe that tonight is the night?" she asks.

"I think tonight *has* to be the night," Ozzy replies, as he focuses on getting his stuff situated.

Patty sets her stuff on the counter and is washing her knife in the sink. "What do you think God is like?" she asks.

Ozzy comes up and puts his arms around her from behind and hugs her. "Baby, I think God is going to be everything we've needed Him to be and more. We just have to get through the hard part… The messy part."

Patty places the knife into the sink and leans back into his warm grasp. "We've waited so long and done everything to serve Him. I can't believe we're about to finally receive His blessings."

Ozzy kisses her on the cheek, and squeezes her tighter. "It's been a long time coming. And God certainly won't overlook all of the work we've done in His name." He separates from her and washes his hands in the sink. Patty grabs a hand towel nearby and dries off her blade.

"We should get started soon," Patty says.

"Yeah. Give me a few minutes and we can get started." he says as he heads upstairs.

25

◇

Other members of the church begin gathering now around the chalk circle, careful not to cross over the line. There are twenty people or so among the group now. Olivia lies on the floor, still unconscious, but begins to stir a bit. Some of the men remove their shirts. One of the much older women is hunched over, walking around with a large wooden bowl and it has a chalky white paste in it. As she walks around, she stops at each person and many of them are scooping handfuls of the paste, while others are a little less liberal with it. The woman is offering the bowl to anyone eager to participate. Her face is completely lathered in this paste and spread down her neck. Her blue eyes, white hair. and white pasty face paint makes her look ghoulish.

As people are getting the paste, they are rubbing it onto their faces. Some of the men are rubbing it onto their bodies as well. Some don't commit to the full face paint look, but choose to write words on their foreheads, or across their chest instead. Some are helping one another apply the paste to each other. One woman writes the word 'LOVE' on her forehead with the paste.

Another has 'PRAISE GOD' written across her chest, over her collar bones, with a cross between her eyes. One guy paints a skull on his face with it. Another guy writes 'ANGEL' on his forehead. Patty joins the circle and the woman comes to her and she scoops a bit of the paste and applies it, exactly how she did with the blood earlier in the evening. Three fingers and she places her middle finger on the bridge of her nose, with a finger on each side of her nose, and she draws straight lines down to the underside of her jaw. She draws this on top of the existing dry blood. She writes 'WELCOME' on her forehead with what is left. Anyone who was wearing one of the masks from the hunt have since discarded them back into a large basket. Now as they move onto the next phase they all prepare to show their true selves.

Olivia lies there with a crowd surrounding her. Everyone is conversing and waiting for Ozzy to come out. Olivia hears the commotion as she is becoming conscious again. She tries to pull her hands down, but before she can, the man watching her with the rope in his lap sees her moving and he pulls on it to raise her hands. She opens her eyes and sees the people around her stop talking to one another and now they're all looking at her, the star of the show. She sees all older men and women with this white paste on their bodies and faces. She also notices the ritualistic drawings on the floor around her just before she closes her eyes really hard and shakes her head. As she opens them again and tries to focus, she feels the rope pull her hands above her head.

She looks up and sees that her hands are tied together and sees the rope strung up, over the rafter. She follows it and sees that a man is about ten feet away, sitting on a picnic table, looking right at her. She tries to stand, but is struggling. Her body is stiff.

She gets one foot planted, and swings her other leg to plant her other foot on the floor. As she digs into the floor to stand, the man pulls a little more on the rope, pulling her up and bringing her hands higher above her head. She gets to her feet and at that point he pulls on it slowly, outstretching her body, so much that she is on her tippy toes to keep the rope from cutting into her skin.

"You're in for a treat now missy!" one man from the crowd says to her, laughing. People in the crowd heckle Olivia while they wait.

The woman with 'LOVE' on her forehead shouts at Olivia, "I know you're scared honey. But it's okay. You should be honored. This is a good thing."

Olivia looks around frantically as people stare at her with hungry eyes and talk to her. She stands there, dancing on her toes, as she hangs there. The weight of her body shifts and causes her to spin slowly. She sees the ghoulish faces in the crowd, all staring at her like she is the star of the show. "Somebody please, just let me go," Olivia begs through a cracking voice accompanied by tears.

"Where ya gonna go? You got some place better to be?" another man says to her, sarcastically.

Pure and concentrated defeat overwhelms Olivia and it shows on her face. She weeps with her head hung low as tears stream down her face. People continue to talk to her and provoke her. "Somebody let me FUCKING GO!" Olivia cries as she raises her head with a look of desperation and anger.

Ozzy begins to walk down the stairs, "Ladies and gentlemen!" Everyone becomes silent as he speaks. He comes down the steps, taking his time, as he fixates his eyes on Olivia. She hangs there looking at him from the corner of her eye. He approaches while the people surrounding her move to let Ozzy through as he steps up to the line drawn on the floor. He is wearing clean dress clothes now as his presentation is completely cleaned up and he has reapplied the nice, charismatic face of the church. He has black dress pants, a clean white, long-sleeve dress shirt with a yellow tie. His hair is wet and slicked back.

"Everyone, I hope you all have taken time to welcome our guest of honor this evening." Ozzy stands there, staring Olivia in the eyes. "This isn't the first time we've performed this ceremony… We've all been in this very room, many, many times before." Ozzy puts his hands behind his back and turns away from the circle and begins to slowly pace around the circle. "Tonight, we begin The Cleansing, once again." Ozzy's footsteps sing along to the symphony of the wooden planks with each slow and heavy step as he speaks. "The others before her, they were young, ungrateful, inconsiderate, undeserving of life, and good representations of everything wrong with this world. But they weren't quite the right offering."

Ozzy captivates everyone as they eat right out of his hand. "We cleansed them. We blessed them. We practiced the routine and adjusted along the way, as we worked to consume their flesh… In the name of God."

Ozzy has everyone's attention as he circles around everyone, with their eyes firmly on Olivia. Olivia continues to try and stand and not move, to no avail.

"Brothers and sisters! Let us begin The Cleansing!" Ozzy commands.

Two women walk away and grab a small bucket with water in it and carry it over to Olivia and they step into the circle, carefully. Olivia stares at them, unsure of what to expect next.

"What's The Cleansing?" Olivia asks the woman beside her.

The woman stares at Olivia's eyes and smiles subtly. "Shhh. Brother Ozzy will explain it all dear," the woman whispers.

Ozzy steps into the circle and drops down to one knee in front of the bucket of water. He holds up two fingers and motions like he is drawing a cross with the fingers upright. "In the name of the one true God Almighty in heaven, soon to be on Earth, I bless this water, and make it divine. Please God, cleanse this girl. Amen."

Everyone watching follows Ozzy's prayer. "Amen!" they all say in unison.

Ozzy stands and backs up, outside of the circle. Olivia's eyes move to everyone around her who moves. One of the women has a big yellow sponge, and she dips it into the bucket. The other woman stands behind Olivia and grabs her waist. "Don't struggle dear. It's okay. We're just gonna get you cleaned up."

Olivia begins to kick and jerk her body wildly. "Get off of me! Get your hands off me! Leave me alone!"

Olivia's pleas are ignored entirely, and she is restrained by the two women. Another woman steps forward and helps to hold her legs. Olivia continues to fight and resist the three women. "Don't you fucking touch me! Don't!" The woman pulls the sponge from the water bucket and begins to put it against Olivia's face. Olivia squirms and emphatically resists as the woman begins to wash her skin. "What are you doing?" Olivia asks through her cries.

The woman continues to lather her with the soapy water, very delicately, as she looks at Olivia with empathy. "Shhh. Shh.

Shh. Shhhhh. It's okay dear." The woman stands in front of Olivia and places her hand on her cheek, intimately, while looking her in the eyes. "It's going to be okay… You're so beautiful. More so than the others."

Olivia, completely restrained, looks into the woman's eyes and spits in her face. "Fuck… YOU!" Olivia screams as she fights harder. Her legs move up and down wildly while the other women try to control her legs. The rope digs into Olivia's wrists more and more as she fights. The woman uses her shirt sleeve to wipe the disrespect from her face, looks up at Olivia and smiles kindly, unphased. Olivia looks at her, gasping heavily as the woman continues to wash her. Olivia is completely exhausted and her fight is quickly fading into shorter bursts of involuntary jerks and flinching, like a fish out of water, flopping around the deck of a boat. "You're all crazy… All of you! You aren't going to be able to get away with this!" she cries.

The woman stares at Olivia and smiles subtly as she is crouched down wringing out the sponge. She stands up and as she is washing Olivia's neck. "Honey… We already have.

26

◇

Two men patrol the road as they walk along the tall grass. One man is wearing a faded Led Zeppelin shirt with bleach stains around the neck and has a large folding knife that he is opening and closing as they walk along. The other man is shirtless with several aged and cheap tattoos on his body. He has a wooden baseball bat that has cloth wrapped around the handle and has seen a game or two. The two men watch out but so far no one has shown up and boredom has led them to off-handed chit-chat as they stroll along the dirt and low cut grass along the roadside.

"Do you think anyone is gonna come?" the bleach-stained-shirt man asks as he plays with his pocket knife.

"I don't know man. We just best keep an eye out," tattooed man replies.

There is silence as the men walk slowly. The guy with the bleach-stained shirt looks at his tattooed friend. "Hey, I got another one."

"Okay…"

"Would you rather…"

"More of this shit?" he scoffs with an eye roll.

"Now just hold on, hold on."

The tattooed man reaches over and pulls the top off of a tall weed. "Alright, go ahead."

"Okay… Would you rather be the smartest person in the world, or the richest person in the world?"

"What kind of question is that supposed to be?"

"Think about it. You can be the smartest person in the world. Like Bill Gates or Elon Musk, one-a-them… Or you can be the richest person in the world… Like–"

"Bill Gates or Elon Musk, okay, okay… I guess… Show me the money you sumbitch!"

They both laugh at the absurdity of the conversation.

"I would be the smartest and earn my money like them rich fuckers," says the bleach-stained shirt guy.

They continue to pace along the road slowly. Mike is in the grass crouched down listening as the men banter about nonsense to kill the time. The men are clearly unsuspecting of anyone and seem to just be assigned to look more imposing then they actually are. *Olivia must be inside.* As the patrolmen are playing would-you-rather, Mike considers his next move. He knows they will see him and there will be confrontation if he comes out or shows himself. He cannot really see them well without standing up and risking being seen. He stays crouched and listens and comes up with his plan. He looks around on the ground and sees that there are clumps of dry mud and some smaller rocks. Mike reaches for the clump of dry mud, but it's more of a large rock in the dirt. He holds it in his hand and listens to their chatter, waiting for his moment.

"Okay, one more," the man with the bleach-stained shirt says.

The tattooed man sighs, annoyed. "…Alright, shoot."

Bleach-stained shirt man perks up. "Okay… See the future? …Or change the past?"

"That one is tricky, yessir. Tricky, tricky,"

"I think I would wanna change the past."

"Yeah? Well, I think that I–"

They hear a noise as Mike tosses the mud clump about ten feet away from where he is in the grass. The mud crashes into the grass and makes enough of a noise to get the two men's attention.

"What the hell was that?" the tattooed man whispers.

"I don't know. Let's check it out."

The two men walk to where the sound came from. The tattooed man with the bat over his shoulder side-steps, looking around cautiously. The bleach-stained shirt man has his knife out, on the offensive as he looks around on high alert. Mike readies himself and waits for the right moment to get the jump on them. The men stop and look around.

"Do you think it could have been a bird?" The bleach-stained shirt man asks.

"I doubt it. Might have been–"

Mike wastes no time as he sneaks up and takes a big swing from behind with the fireplace poker at the man holding the knife, connecting with the right side of his head. The sound of the fireplace poker colliding into his skull breaks the silence of the night like a firecracker. The other man turns around quickly and sees his friend collapse onto the ground as Mike stands there gripping the fireplace poker with both hands. Mike looks at the tattooed man with the baseball bat and takes a step toward him.

The tattooed man holds the bat up defensively. "Oh you done fucked up now boy." He holds it out in one hand like it's a sword. Mike walks toward him and the man takes a stab at him with the weapon. Mike knocks the bat down with the fireplace poker and the tattooed man steps back and lifts the bat to take a big swing. Before he gets the bat up enough to get any meaningful momentum behind his swing, Mike has already swung the fireplace poker and connected with his ribs. The tattooed man immediately drops the bat and drops his arm down to protect himself. Mike takes another swing and hits the tattooed man's shoulder. The man drops to one knee and Mike prepares his next swing and rotates his shoulders, then brings the poker behind his back and brings it down from over his head with a manly roar. The tattooed man holds his other arm up to block the hit and the curved, pointy part of the fireplace poker goes right through his hand.

The tattooed man's face says everything that his voice doesn't. His eyes open wide with fear as he sees it go through his hand as he was protecting himself. His mouth opens to scream but nothing comes out. Eventually a quiet squeal comes out and as Mike goes to pull the poker back for another swing but it is stuck in his hand. As he pulls, the tattooed man is caught off balance and falls to the ground on his stomach and the poker tears out of his hand. He rolls over on his back "Owww, my hand! You fucked up my hand! You motherfucker!" he cries.

Mike looks around, still on the offensive, and sees the man in the bleach-stained shirt who he hit in the side of the head moving around to get up. He gets up holding his head, and stretches his neck and tries to shake off the hit, pretending he didn't just get walloped by an iron rod. He sees Mike standing there with the fireplace poker and looks for his knife, stumbling as he bends down and gets it. He points it at Mike while he is holding his head with the other hand. The tattooed man is still on the ground kicking and crying while he holds his hand against his chest. Mike takes a defensive swing at the man in the bleach-stained shirt. The man backs up and Mike takes a second swing, this time a little harder, and as he misses, the man lunges forward and slices his arm. Mike takes a step back, looks at his arm, and sees it's a clean slice and hasn't even begun to bleed yet.

Mike looks back at the man holding the knife and rushes at him. He has the poker in one hand and uses his other hand to grab the wrist of the man's hand that is holding the knife. Bleach-stained shirt man drops the knife when Mike twists the wrist in a way that it is not meant to move. Mike quickly gets himself behind the man and puts the fireplace poker against his throat. Mike pulls on it with both hands, putting as much pressure on it as he can. He leans his body against the bleach-stained shirt man and kicks the back of his knees to force him onto the ground. Once the man is on his knees and flailing his arms trying to hit Mike, Mike locks in the chokehold with the fireplace poker and is wrenching back. Mike only sees red as he applies what he intends to be fatal pressure. The tattooed man on the ground holding his hand sees this and he staggers to get to his feet. He begins to stumble over to try and stop Mike.

Mike maintains the choke as the tattooed man bends down to pick up the baseball bat. Mike releases the chokehold and the beach-stained shirt man falls onto the ground, gasping for every bit of precious air. Mike swings the fireplace poker, slamming it down onto the tattooed man's back while he is bent over. The man crumbles onto the ground, shrieking in pain. Mike is in absolute control and takes slow steps toward him as he squirms and thrashes on the ground after taking that hit.

Mike drops the fireplace poker and he bends over slowly and picks up the knife, admiring it. Mike's demeanor has completely changed, as motivation to save Olivia is paramount, and he recognizes that he has already crossed lines tonight that he may never come back from. Both men lie on the ground, at his mercy. Mike steps over the tattooed man and he rolls him onto his back. Mike drops down, on top of him, and uses one hand to pin down his non-injured hand.

"Please. Please don't kill me. I quit. I quit! I just wanna go home. O-Ozzy gives, h-he the orders. I-I j-just do what I'm told."

Mike squeezes the man's hand that is pinned down and shows his clenched teeth, leaning over the scared man. "We just wanted to go home too!" he roars.

The tattooed man pleads for his life from a very vulnerable position as Mike looks him in the eyes. "Listen, listen, listen, I-I can get you cash. We, *WE* can get you cash… It don't have to go down like this, we can–" Mike has heard enough. He unleashes a flurry of short range stabs with the knife into the tattooed man's chest, sternum, and stomach. It's a mess of stabs, as clearly Mike has no desire to be precise. The tattooed man screams for his life before he quickly begins to choke on his curdling blood. Blood bursts from his mouth with each violent cough, as he suffers, fading quickly while Mike stands over him, with a firm grip on the bloody knife, watching his last gasp for air before he is gone.

The bleached-shirt man is still catching his breath as he raises up to see this beast that Mike has let out. He gets to his feet and starts to run the other way, but he is stumbling and not running as fast as his effort might suggest. He begins shouting. "Help!… Help! …We need back up! FUBAR! FUBAR!"

Mike walks quickly toward him as he drops the knife and picks up the baseball bat in one swift motion as he moves. He grips the wrapped handle of the wooden bat firmly as he begins to lightly jog after him. "Help me! God please! God! Fuck! Fuck!" the man with the bleach-stained shirt says as he has already begun hyperventilating. He turns back to see Mike right on his heels. "No! Please!" he begs as Mike takes a running swing with one hand and clobbers this man in the face with the wooden bat. The man does a backflip and lands on his back like he was clotheslined by a professional wrestler after the hit.

Mike stands beside him as he rolls onto his stomach and starts to crawl, spitting blood onto the ground. Mike raises the bat high over his head. "You know… That felt like a foul… I think I should get another swing!" Mike brings the bat down as he swings for the fences, and caves in the man's skull instantly. It is a no-doubt, out of the park shot! He takes a second swing to really put an exclamation mark on the one-sided brawl. Mike stands there winded, bloody, and transformed, holding onto the baseball bat with one hand, trying to calm himself. Adrenaline is ripping through his body as he looks around at the scene he is leaving behind. Two men slain in the grass, on the side of the road is not how Mike saw his night turning out at all. With the baseball bat at his disposal, he peeks out of the grass and comes out to cross the road. No one within sight, no cars oncoming from either direction as he jogs across the road. He creeps past the gas station, locking his eyes onto the barn as he approaches it. The two large barn doors on the front are now closed but a light can be seen through the cracks of the doors.

He sneaks up to the barn, undetected, and he stands against the outside wall. He puts his ear against the door and he can hear Olivia's cries over the sound of other voices.

27

The Cleansing

Mike hears the desperation in Olivia's crying and fighting and knows he has to get inside or come up with something fast. He continues to listen and inches closer to the opening of the two doors and begins to watch inside through the quarter inch vertical opening. With his very limited visibility, he sees people crowded around Olivia, and can see her tied up, and suspended while people try to restrain her and appear to be washing her. He sees Ozzy outside of the crowd, pacing with his hands behind his back. Mike watches, unnoticed as everything is happening inside, while he tries to come up with a plan of some sort.

Olivia crying and sobbing is the soundtrack for the evening as this seemingly routine ritual carries on. The woman with the sponge delicately cleans Olivia. Olivia's struggle begins to be less active and more defeated. All of her efforts to survive have still led her to this point as she hangs there feeling hopeless. As Ozzy paces patiently behind the circle of participants, he is thinking about what he is to say to his followers. Ozzy looks to his left and looks at Olivia as he stops. He walks in between people and steps over the line drawn on the floor and into the circle. The women holding onto Olivia let her go and take several steps back and out of the circle. The woman cleaning her places the sponge into the bucket. She stands in front of Olivia with a proud and unsettling smile. "It's time sweetie… Be free."

Olivia stands on the tips of her toes, suspended by rope with her arms outstretched above her head. She tries to widen her feet on the floor to keep from spinning. Ozzy steps in front of her and he puts his hands on her shoulders and turns her to face him. He looks at her closely up and down as Olivia looks at him with tears in her eyes, completely exhausted.

"Miss Margaret got ya nice and cleaned up. I think we're ready to begin The Cleansing now." Ozzy takes a few steps back, keeping his eyes fixated on Olivia the entire time. He holds his right hand out to his side. Patty comes forward and places a roll of duct tape in his hand. He unravels a strip about the length of his hand from palm to fingertips then hands the roll back to Patty. "Thank you dear." With the tape in his hand, he walks over to Olivia. "You're gonna need this hun," He carefully puts the tape over her mouth and brushes his hand across it to make sure it is secured tight. Olivia jerks her head and fights but her efforts to resist are minimal compared to earlier. Olivia tries to scream but her voice is muffled now by the tape.

Ozzy steps back, just outside of the circle. The crowd moves aside in both directions to give him space. "Ladies and gentlemen… Brothers and sisters… Tonight is the night that we celebrate. A night to commemorate. A night to welcome… God…" He looks around the room, pausing for theatrics. "We welcome God not just into our hearts… But into our home." The people in the room all look at him in adoration. Olivia watches him, exhaling from her nose furiously in wide-eyed horror as beads of sweat drip off her forehead. Ozzy looks back at Olivia. "You seem scared," He takes steps toward her. "Are you scared?" He smiles and tenderly brushes the back of his hand down her cheek. Olivia pulls her head back as he laughs to himself. "You really are beautiful. Quite perfect actually. You shouldn't be scared though… no, no, no. You should feel honored. You're about to be the key to God finally gracing us with His presence. Because of you, we're finally going to know heaven on earth."

"My brothers and sisters… They are expressing their devotion to God and what we represent. They wear the ash and burnt remains of all of the past offerings who weren't enough for God to answer our calls." As he is giving his sermon, the woman with the paste bowl comes over to him. Ozzy dips his index finger into the bowl and he proceeds to draw a cross on his forehead, then turns to the crowd. "Brothers and sisters, this is the first cleansing we've been able to perform in some time now. It's been about nine months, I do recall."

Ozzy paces the room as he is addressing the entire group. "Earlier today, we were just driving back from running errands. Nothing interesting. We were nearly home when this group of young, entitled, and quite frankly, disrespectful kids thought it would be a great idea to poke the bear for their amusement. Jasper and Cliff wanted to respond right then but I calmed them down in the van. We let them go on about their business. But then, at the gas station… Well I seen't what these boys were really all about and, well, I just couldn't help but to think… Is this… Is this God trying to talk to me? Could this be God saying He wants another offering and that these people might be *just right*? It's like God gift-wrapped them and put a bow on it and was begging us to perform The Cleansing and call out to Him again… Like a sign, something divine. Well I would be a fool to not listen to God, am I right?"

The crowd all responds simultaneously, "Right!"

"Well, from there it was obvious. Simple! I have never seen a light so bright, ever in my life! Not at any point on my journey to find God and true, rich, enlightenment have I ever seen a sign so obvious, so blinding. We had to work fast to get them here. We had to make a statement that their disregard for others is not okay. We had to use their lives to entice God… As we prepare the flesh for consumption, we will pray together, brothers and sisters. We will devour her cleansed body and offer her heart to God. Once we're finished, we will be on our way to the prolonged preservation of the youth we have left. And in that moment when God walks into this place and offers us His blessings… we will be grateful, and we will praise Him. We will be His swords of justice, His angel army, if He so desires, and we will continue to eradicate the ungrateful, filthy, and wicked from this place!" Ozzy speaks passionately and with such conviction.

"Everyone!" Ozzy stands with his arms spread wide as he turns to face his devotees. "Make preparations for His arrival as we complete The Cleansing. Tonight we feast!" He walks over to Olivia and stands in front of her, staring intently into her eyes. He holds out his right hand. One of the women in the circle scatters to retrieve a decorative glass bowl with water in it. She places it delicately in his hand. He brings the bowl close to his chest, bows his head as he says a prayer to himself. "In the name of the Father, the Son, and the Mother, I ask that You bless this water. May Your blessings be used to expel any and all impurities in this world." He motions his left hand in the shape of a cross as he concludes the short prayer. He dips the tips of his fingers into the bowl and flicks water onto Olivia's face. She winces as he does this, squirming and dancing around on her tiptoes. The rope is digging into her wrists as she continues to hang and keep feet on the floor to relieve some of the tension.

Ozzy turns and hands off the bowl of holy water to the woman who brought it to him. She takes it and hustles off to the kitchen area. Ozzy stands with his arms crossed and a hand on his chin as he stares at Olivia. Olivia still lets out muffled sounds as she anxiously watches Ozzy stare back at her.

"I think it's time. Bring out the throne!" Ozzy commands. With urgency, four men leave the circle and head up the stairs to the upper level of the barn. "Let us sing songs of praise while we welcome Him to take His rightful place on Earth."

The people begin to chant. The chants start off messy and unorganized but they adjust their timing to become in sync with one another.

"Wicked souls, all shall fall, God will come and save us all.

Eat the flesh, live in His grace, We beg You God to take Your place."

The chant carries on through the room as the four men are upstairs. Mike sits outside watching still through the crack of the front doors. Ozzy turns to the crowd and is pantomiming as if he is orchestrating a choir. The four men come to the edge of the stairs carrying a large wooden seat. They slowly walk down the steps with the large fixture.

Ozzy claps with a big smile on his face. "Yes! YES! Beautiful!"

The men get off the stairs and walk near the circle on the floor. People spread apart to make room. The chair is gently placed on the floor, just in front of Olivia. The chair has beautiful woodwork with incredible details that a very talented artist would have done. It is polished and shining, the upholstery looks soft and gives this seat a very luxurious look, and it looks like it does not belong in this setting at all.

The men who carried the throne return to the circle and join in with the chanting, as they become a little louder, and a little more intense. A few women begin placing lit candles throughout the barn. Once they are finished, the lights are turned off and the scene is set with candlelight, the mantra, and Ozzy standing beside the gorgeous throne, staring at Olivia as she screams into the sticky side of the duct tape. She kicks wildly as the chanting becomes even more intense. They offer praise to God, dawning the ashes of their past victims on their skin.

Ozzy steps out of the circle and it appears his work is done, and he joins in with the chanting. Patty and Margaret step into the circle. Margaret is carrying a cookie sheet with rubbing alcohol, a rag, a bowl of water, and a small selection of knives. Olivia tries to kick Patty and Margaret but they are just barely out of reach. Patty takes the rubbing alcohol and she pours it on her hands. She lathers it on like it's lotion. Patty turns to Olivia and looks her up and down. The chanting ensues as everyone watches Patty, who seems to be the star performer now. Patty looks out to the people and she nods at a woman to come to her. The woman steps into the circle. "I need you to hold her legs for this part," Patty instructs.

The woman nods and walks behind Olivia. Olivia tries to fight and kicks but the woman just catches one leg at a time and holds her still. Olivia is suspended and being held up by the woman from the crowd who held her when she was being given the sponge bath. The woman crouches down, getting on one knee as she hugs Olivia's thighs, just above the knees.

Patty walks over to Olivia with the rubbing alcohol. She looks her up and down once more. She zeroes in on her right leg and splashes rubbing alcohol onto the front of her right thigh. Olivia squirms and is thrusting her hips as hard as she can, like a bucking horse, as she makes muffled noises that go largely ignored. Everyone who is watching is fixated on the mantra that is being repeated passionately by everyone outside of the circle. Patty begins to look at the knives on the cookie sheet that Margaret is holding. She grabs a large chef's knife and puts it down quickly. She admires a filet knife for a little longer before also putting that down. She then picks up a box cutter and places her thumb on the sliding button to extend the breakaway blade that hides inside of the cheap plastic, yellow casing. "This will do," she says as she nods.

Olivia's fear has her in full panic-mode. *Patty must be completely insane.* Patty grabs the rag and dips a small part in the bowl of water. She walks over to Olivia with the box cutter in one hand and the wet rag in the other. Patty stands close to Olivia and their eyes meet. "You're gonna wanna be real still sweetheart, this is gonna hurt… *a lot.*" She gets down onto her knees and puts the rag on her shoulder. She extends the blade and begins to size up the skin. Olivia squirms even more, making more noise than before, knowing exactly what is about to happen.

Mike watches and knows he needs to do something, but also knows he can't reveal himself because there is a small mob inside that would descend upon him on sight. Mike moves away from the doors quickly and goes around the side of the barn. He pulls the gun out of the back of his waistband and looks at it. He doesn't want to waste the bullets since he only has two. "Dammit!" he mumbles under his breath, as he puts the gun back in his waistband. On the side area of the barn, there are some stadium seats, a row of four that are connected. There are some cinder blocks stacked, a pair of metal trash cans with lids, and some gas canisters, along with some common gardening equipment lying on the ground. There is an old farm tractor parked nearby. He hops up into the driver seat and is looking around and right in the ignition is a key with a bottle opener keychain, shaped like a palm tree.

Inside the barn, Patty takes the blade and starts digging into Olivia's thigh, slicing about two inches in a straight line. Olivia's screams in excruciating pain as the sound of her suffering is muffled. Patty continues to cut and Olivia tenses up and isn't doing much moving or screaming now. Patty removes a square chunk of flesh from Olivia's thigh and stands up. She holds it up and turns to the crowd showing it off as everyone claps, but the chanting does not stop. She places the slab of human flesh onto the cookie sheet. "Season that up," she says as she goes back to her knees and uses the rag to clean up the bleeding.

As Patty prepares to make another cut, suddenly outside a motor fires up and gets everyone's attention. The chanting slows and then altogether stops. Ozzy draws his gun and heads to the door. The circle dissipates as Jasper, Virgil, and another man with a mangy beard join Ozzy. "Be careful. We don't know what's out there waiting for us," Ozzy cautions the three men. Jasper opens the barn doors just enough to be able to slide out. Virgil and the bearded man follow.

Mike hops down from the tractor moments before Jasper opens the barn doors. The motor hums and rattles loudly and he is no longer able to hear the chanting inside. He runs to the back of the barn and looks around for a place to hide quickly. He still has the baseball bat with him in one hand. He sees a few tall stacks of old tires near some tall grass and he scurries off to hide behind the tires. He is in the dark and not visible at all but he is able to see through the tires enough to tell if anyone is coming his way. Jasper comes out first, hatchet in hand, and he looks around. "Where ya at?" Jasper shouts. Virgil comes out also, along with the bearded man carrying a pipe.

Jasper climbs up onto the tractor and gets in the seat. He looks around for a moment and takes the key out of the ignition, shutting off the loud motor. Virgil stands beside the tractor. "You guys see anything?" he asks. Jasper hops down and walks out toward the front of the barn. Virgil stands around, just posturing more than anything. The bearded man slowly creeps toward the back of the barn. He walks slowly and is on the lookout for anything. Mike is watching him and waiting to make a move. The bearded man walks slowly but as he is passing right in front of Mike, Mike pushes a tire stack over and they fall on top of him. The bearded man is caught off guard and knocked to the ground. Tires bounce and roll in different directions. Mike rushes over to him and gives him a kick to the face before he even sees Mike. Virgil sees the tires rolling and hears the noise and is walking back.

Mike pulls the bearded man to his feet by the back of his shirt and he begins to choke him with the baseball bat. The bearded man flails his arms, trying to hit Mike or at the very least loosen up the chokehold. Mike applies more pressure as he sees

Virgil walking toward him. "Over here! He's over here!" Virgil shouts.

Mike pulls the bearded man as he walks backwards and violently slings him onto the ground. Before the bearded man can get his balance, Mike winds up and takes a big swing at his head. He connects and the bat smashes against his face. Blood spews out following the hit as the man hits the dirt and is out cold. Mike turns to Virgil who is coming near him. Jasper is also walking back quickly. Mike draws the revolver and points it at Virgil. "Stay right there! I'll blow your brains all over the motherfucker behind you!" Mike places his thumb on the hammer and pulls it back, ready to fire.

"Whoa. Take it easy kid, let's just talk," Virgil says.

Jasper walks up and stands beside Virgil. "That's what's wrong with this country. Guns are just out of control. Why don't you put the gun down, boy?" Jasper suggests.

As Mike stands there with the gun aimed, he feels something pressed against his lower back. He looks over his shoulder and before he can react. "At! At! At! Turn on back around now son. Drop the weapon," Patty says as she holds a rifle against Mike's back. She ambushes him from the back. Mike drops the baseball bat while still aiming the gun at Virgil.

"The other weapon," Patty says.

"Not a chance," Mike replies firmly.

Patty nudges the nose of the rifle against his back. "If you don't drop that gun right now I'll blow your spine through your stomach. I said drop it, boy!"

"If you shoot me, I'll get at least one shot off into the old fuck's head," Mike snaps.

As soon as Mike says that, Ozzy comes around the corner and has Olivia with her hands still tied in front of her, with a fistful of hair in the other hand. "Let her go!" Mike shouts.

Ozzy laughs as he walks closer. "Now why would I do that? Come on kid, put the gun down. Don't make me go and do something awful to your little lady friend here."

"I'm not dropping anything. Let her go. We're leaving," Mike says with extreme confidence.

Ozzy's face turns serious. "You interrupted our ceremony there. That was real fuckin' cute." Ozzy draws his glock and aims it at the side of Olivia's head and he pulls her hair, jerking her hair closer to him. She screams, hardly making a sound as you can see the fear in her eyes as Ozzy looks at Mike with a deadly serious face. "If you don't put the gun down, I'll put her down."

28

◇

Mike stands there with Patty's gun at his back as he points a revolver at Virgil who stands there with his hands up looking at Ozzy. Ozzy has a glock pressed against the side of Olivia's head while Jasper stands there, holding a hatchet, like an eager attack dog just itching to chase the rabbit. Olivia looks at Mike with tears on her face and fear in her eyes. With a chunk of skin carved out of her thigh, the blood continues to run down her leg.

"What's it gonna be, boy?" Ozzy asks, firmly.

Mike and Olivia's eyes meet, with her desperate to speak, if even to just cry for a moment. He looks at Virgil, then over to Jasper who is ready to rush at Mike. Mike feels Patty press the nose of the rifle against his lower back, as if to nudge him forward.

"Go on… Drop it," Patty says calmly.

Mike turns his head slightly and tries to look at Patty out of the corner of his eye. "You shoot me, I empty the gun. Do you really want to take that chance? Just let us go."

"Hmph, it seems you're outnumbered. What makes you think there is any scenario where you leave here alive, let alone both of you?" Patty asks flatly.

Ozzy bites on his bottom lip and looks away, visibly frustrated. 'Listen. I'm already feeling reeeeally moody about what you guys did to our brothers, and I reeeeally was looking forward to completing The Cleansing and bringing God into our home," he says, with his patience breaking, "but you're making it really difficult to not spray her brains all over the grass," he snaps as he jerks Olivia's head around as he becomes more animated with the violent, unpredictable tone in his voice. Olivia cries and screams into the duct tape.

Mike snickers. "You think killing a woman is going to bring God? Here? You're a bat shit crazy redneck in an oversized shed behind a filthy gas station. Are you that delusional?" Mike laughs a little more to himself as he insults Ozzy. "Why– Why on Earth– Would God, the creator– Why would God show Himself here? Of all of the places–" Mike continues through laughter.

"Watch your mouth boy," Ozzy warns with seething rage in his eyes.

"WHY? She said it herself. We're already dead right? You're going to do what you're going to do regardless. What's to stop me from blowing pork chop here into bacon bits?" Mike replies, laughing even harder.

"Just kill her! We can deal with him!" Jasper growls.

"Quiet!" Ozzy barks as Jasper falls silent. Ozzy yanks Olivia's head back really hard. With the gun still in his hand, he reaches up with his fingertips and peels a corner of the tape off. He gets a good grip and tears the tape off of her mouth, very rough and very quickly. Olivia lets out a screeching yelp as she stands there, in agonizing pain. Ozzy lets her head go, but puts the gun against her head again. "Honey, please talk some sense into your friend here. His mouth is about to get you both killed."

Olivia stands there, subdued as she stretches her mouth. "Do it! Shoot him!" she bites, with anger spewing from her cracked and raspy voice.

Ozzy grabs her hair and yanks her head back again. "You stupid, stupid girl," he looks at Mike scratching his forehead with the barrel of the gun. "My patience is just about gone, drop the damn gun. You ain't no John Wayne, and this ain't no–"

Mike instinctively side steps to his right and slaps down the gun at his back, catching Patty by surprise. The rifle goes off and the bullet hits the gas canister on the ground beside the barn, causing an instantaneous explosion. Mike kicks Patty's ankle, sweeping her off her feet as she slams onto her back, still clutching the rifle. Jasper, Ozzy, Virgil, and Olivia are all on the ground from the explosion. Jasper is on fire and rolling around yelling. Virgil is on the ground stunned and Ozzy is on fire, but not nearly the way Jasper is. Olivia is face down and tucking her knees in to try and stand.

Mike quickly kicks the rifle out of Patty's hands and then delivers a stomp to her face. As his foot connects, the back of her head bangs against the hard dirt. Her eyes close and her neck bounces right back up like a spring. Mike delivers another stomp, this time ever harder, and with more intent and better balance behind it. Her nose begins to bleed and run down her cheeks and her mouth as she raises her arms up to try and block a third kick to the face. Mike drops to his knees and grabs her by the throat and raises her up and slams her down, banging her head on the ground once more. She grabs onto his wrist but her grip is broken on the next impact as Mike repeatedly knocks the back of her head against the ground. Her eyes roll back in her head and Mike stops and lets go. He stands up, staggering backwards, exasperated and overcome with fury. Patty rolls over onto her side slowly and puts her hand on the back of her head.

Mike looks around, and sees Jasper on fire, rolling around. Ozzy is just getting to his feet and is smacking his shirt sleeve to put out a small fire on his arm. He sees Jasper in pain as he rolls around and immediately goes over to try and put the fire out. As he pats him down and tries to stop him from moving erratically, he sees just how bad it is. His shirt is tattered and smoking still and he has some bad burns on his arms and back and the hair on the back and right side of his head is burned up. The right side of his face is red and swelling. Jasper lies on his back with his arms and legs tensed up as he screams wildly in pain.

"Hold still, will ya? Let me get a look atcha!" Ozzy says, assertively to Jasper. "Ah hell! We're gonna need to get you some medical attention, ASAP."

Olivia gets to her feet, with her hands still tied, while Ozzy tends to Jasper. "Go! Run!" she shouts as she runs over to Mike. Mike looks at Ozzy and begins to follow Olivia as they run around to the back of the barn. They are out of sight now as they hurriedly look for a place to hide, a place to run, or anything that gives them a better chance of getting out of this place alive. The area behind the barn is cluttered, but with a clearing to move around freely. Against the back of the barn is a makeshift shelving structure with a variety of outdoor tools. There are containers and jugs of chemicals, like weedkiller, pest control, cleaning materials, several gallon jugs of bleach, and a tray with some small rodents that are already skinned. Their pelts are laid out deliberately on another shelf and appear to include a couple of raccoons, a squirrel, and an opossum. There is also a small fox that is posted to the backside of the barn, pinned up with a machete.

There is a charcoal grill with a smoker near this shelving piece, and also a small fire pit made out of an old oil drum that is cut down low and has paver bricks stacked up around it, with large tree trunk chunks laid out around it for seating. On the firepit there is a fresh pig that is hog tied and hanging from a pipe over the pit. There is a tool shed across the clearing. Mike and Olivia look around, panicked.

"What do we do? *What do we do*?" Mike asks Olivia.

"Find something! Run! Hide! I don't know! Help me get this rope off!" Olivia replies, as she bites on the knot of the rope trying to loosen it.

Mike goes over to the shelf and is looking around, urgently, when he notices the fox on the wall, pulls the machete out, and throws the fox onto the ground.

"I got it. Hold still!" Mike says as he races over to Olivia with the machete in hand. She holds her hands away from her body, with her palms up, trying to pull her hands away from one another to create space for Mike to cut the rope.

"Hurry, hurry, hurry!" Olivia begs. Mike positions the blade up and carefully cuts in a sawing motion until the rope is severed. Olivia's hands break free and she rubs her wrists with immediate relief. Her wrists are red and bruised with rope burn and riddled with cuts where the rope had dug into her skin for so long.

"They're coming!" Mike says, as he pushes Olivia. "Go! Hide!" he says as he runs over to the back of the shed.

29

The Devil's Playground

Mike hides, waiting for someone to come around the corner, as he grips the machete tightly, prepared to go down swinging. Olivia looks around, under pressure, when sees the shed and goes inside. Darkness pours into the inside of the shed but she sees a pair of orange five-gallon buckets on the right side when she opens the door. They have bones in them and it is indistinguishable if they are animal or human. As she looks up and tries to look further in, she sees a workbench with a dead body laid on top of it. There are what appears to be taxidermy tools hanging on a pegboard above the workbench.

"They're in the back. Nowhere to go! Find them!" Ozzy says in the distance. Without hesitation, Olivia goes into the shed and pulls the door shut. In total darkness, she backs away from the door slowly, never taking her eyes off of the shed doors. As she backs into the workbench, she crouches down and hides underneath it. She sits for a moment, scared for her life and realizes that it's going to take a miracle to escape these people who clearly have been doing this for a while. She worries for Mike who is still outside.

Olivia tries to listen closely to what is happening outside and hears Ozzy's voice from far away. Her eyes begin to adjust to the darkness and she sees a wheelbarrow to her right. She cannot help but to fixate her eyes to it as she is listening. As she stares a bit longer she sees that inside the wheelbarrow there is another body. She covers her mouth to keep from screaming. She has locked eyes with a dead body that stares back at her. A literal dead stare pierces through her soul as she sits beneath this workbench, hidden and horrified.

Meanwhile, Patty has got back to her feet after being stomped in the face multiple times. She is angry as she looks at Jasper and Ozzy. She spits blood onto the ground and bends down to snatch the rifle up. Jasper sits up and is in rough shape but able to move around. "To hell with this. I'm going to kill them both, right now!" Jasper says. He looks around for his hatchet. Ozzy picks it up and hands it to him.

"Are you sure you're in shape to do this brother?" Ozzy asks.

"Where are they?" Jasper asks as he snatches the hatchet from Ozzy. "I'm sick of you dickin' around. You're so fixed on God that you can't see what these kids are doin' to us!" he bites.

"Which is exactly why this can't be for nothing!" Ozzy snaps back. "Jasper, you need medical attention. Let me take care of-"

"What you're doin' ain't workin' Oz. This needs to end. I'm going to kill them!" Jasper growls with his skin still smoking.

Virgil slowly moves around and sits up. He looks disoriented as he is looking around. He sees Patty, face bloodied, Ozzy with a gun in his hand, and Jasper standing up, injured badly. Pieces of a metal gas can are still burning on the ground and embers blowing in the light breeze. "What– what just happened?" Virgil asks as he sits, confused.

Ozzy goes over to Virgil and extends his hand to help him up. "Let's get you on your feet big guy." Virgil takes Ozzy's hand and he is pulled to his feet. Virgil looks around, a little dazed as Ozzy brushes off the dirt on the front of his shirt.

"Where are they?" Virgil asks.

Ozzy looks over to Jasper and Patty, then back to Virgil. "They're round' back. We need to make sure they don't get away. There is only one way out."

"Let's find 'em then," Virgil slurs.

"You sure you're okay?" Patty asks as she wipes blood from her nose.

Ozzy puts his hand on Virgil's shoulder and pauses for a second. "We need to cut them off out front. They might try to sneak out the other side of the compound. I'm gonna go inside and grab a more …*personal* weapon. Patty, you try to flank 'em round' the other side." Patty nods in agreement and walks toward the front, loading another round into the chamber of the rifle.

"Come on Virgil. Let's go do God's work," Jasper says as he slaps his knuckles against Virgil's belly, in a playful sort of way.

Virgil catches a glimpse of Jasper's leathery and burnt face. "Brother, you might wanna sit this one out. You aren't lookin' so good," he says through disgust.

"I'll live. We still got work to do! We're in too deep now," Jasper replies, unbothered by the obvious.

"Alright. Let's go then," Virgil says, walking toward the back.

"Alright then! Let's end this, boys! I'll just be a second," Ozzy says, putting his gun in the back of his waistband and heading toward the front. Virgil walks toward the back, along the side of the barn. As he is walking with a little more urgency in his pace, he approaches the back of the building. Mike stands on the other side, out of sight, waiting. Mike hears the footsteps creeping closer, gripping the machete handle tight as he holds it close to his chest, with his back to the wall.

Virgil comes up and suddenly all he hears is a roaring yell.

"Yagghh!" Mike jumps out from around the corner and swings the machete hard and wild, hitting Virgil's left shoulder with enough brute force to cut clean through if it weren't for the bone stopping it. "Motherfucking, SHIT! Ow!" Virgil cries.

Mike pulls the machete back for another massive swing as Virgil staggers back. The swing misses and the machete is implanted into the side of the barn. Virgil stumbles and falls to the ground as he looks down to see the blood pouring out from the top of his left bicep, close to the shoulder. He starts to panic at the sight of all of the blood. Virgil looks up while he is scooting away from Mike when he sees Jasper rushing Mike with the hatchet in his hand. Jasper swings the hatchet at Mike as he is trying to pull the planted machete from the barn. Mike sees the hatchet coming at him and he falls back to avoid the attack. Mike scurries backwards on the ground as he scoots across the dirt. Jasper pulls the hatchet from the barn after missing what would have no doubt been a killing blow.

Mike tries to jump up to his feet and before he can create any distance, Jasper pounces him with much less explosive energy than he once had but still not so weak to not send Mike crashing back onto the ground. Olivia hears the fighting and remains hidden. Virgil sits on the ground holding his shoulder as he bleeds, trying to get to his feet. Jasper is on top of Mike and drives his forearm into Mike's face, pinning him down very aggressively. Jasper raises the hatchet up and before he could get stabilized enough to get a good swing, Mike digs his feet into the ground and thrusts his hips up in an explosive way that causes Jasper to fall forward, allowing Mike to get out from under him. Mike jumps to his feet and gets in a defensive position. Jasper pops back up quickly also.

"Today ain't cho day, boy… This is the end of the road for you," Jasper hisses as he stares into Mike's eyes in a defensive position just a few feet apart. The two stand ready to fight as they circle. Jasper spins the hatchet in his hands while he licks and bites on his bottom lip.

"If you're gonna do something' then do something'!" Mike barks.

Jasper stares back at him with focused anger. "You gon' wish you kept runnin' now," he says as he steps forward with a weak swing of the hatchet.

"COME ON! Whatchu got boy?" Jasper taunts as he lunges forward with another swing of the hatchet, this time with a little more umph behind it. "Heh heh heh, you ain't got nothin', I can see ya scared. I see the wheels turnin' in ya head," Jasper toys as he twirls his finger around his ear slowly. Jasper takes another step forward and swings the hatchet again, only this time Mike steps to the side and grabs Jasper's forearm and pulls his momentum after the swing in the opposite direction. Jasper's legs crossover and go every which way, throwing him off balance.

While Mike has a firm grip on Jasper's forearm, he pulls him in close and drives a big knee strike into his stomach. Jasper hunches over immediately after having the wind knocked out of him. As he hunches over, Mike drives the same knee into the side of his head. Jasper crumbles to the ground, but Mike is still holding onto his forearm. Mike twists his arm and puts pressure on the elbow in the wrong direction and Jasper drops the hatchet.

Mike lets go of Jasper and as he goes for the hatchet, Jasper races to kick it out of the way, and the hatchet spins and skips across the ground, about ten feet away into the grass. Mike then drops down and puts Jasper in a side headlock and cranks back on his head, causing Jasper to flatten out onto his stomach completely. "AAAGGGHHH!" Mike howls as he is trying to rip Jasper's head off of his shoulders. As Mike is trying to finish off Jasper, Virgil walks up and reaches down and grabs Mike by the back of his shirt collar, and he pulls Mike off so hard that his shirt tears. Mike gets to his feet and pulls his shirt off and throws it in Virgil's face. Virgil slaps the shirt away and Mike charges at him and tackles him, knocking him right onto his ass. Virgil's large frame slams down and knocks the wind out of him. Virgil's shoulder is still bleeding heavily as he lies on his back.

Olivia is still in the shed as all of this fighting ensues and she is hearing everything as it happens. She walks up to the doors, peering through the wood but has a very limited view and cannot really see Mike out there, she just hears him grunting and yelling. She looks around the shed and sees some tools hanging on hooks, just above the body that is in the wheelbarrow. She is hurrying now to see what tools there are. She can see that one item is a leaf blower, another is a weed eater, and there is an auger. She feels around the base of the equipment and can feel the ripcords and makes the assumption that these are probably gas powered. As she is focusing on the auger and its wide and awkward-looking handles, her eyes adjust even more to the dark as she realizes that the person in the wheelbarrow is Nate.

"Oh my g-!" she shrieks, covering her mouth to keep from being heard. She falls onto her knees and stares at Nate as she breaks down once more. Tears streaming down her cheek. Exhausted and in survival-mode, with a restored thirst for justice, she gets back to her feet and reaches for a tool. *No time for mourning now.*

Mike climbs on top of Virgil and starts to go to work on his face with a series of left forearm blows that will get anyone's attention. As Mike reaches back for another blow, Jasper grabs Mike's wrist and as Mike turns to look back, Jasper delivers a fist into Mike's jaw, sending him crashing to the ground, rolling away from Jasper and Virgil. Jasper is quick and angry, like a starved, rabid dog, and Mike is just fresh meat.

Jasper rushes over and puts his boots into Mike's lower back, followed by several more kicks to a vulnerable and grounded Mike. Mike rolls onto his stomach and hands to try and get to his feet and defend himself but the kicks keep coming, and now he is getting it in the stomach and ribs. Jasper stays on him, much more aggressive than he has been all night.

Virgil is back on his feet and angry. He walks over to Mike and reaches down and pulls him to his feet. Mike stumbles around while Virgil struggles to do much with his shoulder injury, but hopes to subdue Mike enough to get the killing blow. Mike is dazed and struggling to stand. Mike smiles with blood in his mouth as he looks Virgil in the eyes and he spits in his face.

"You motherfucker!" Virgil screams as he pushes Mike into the wall of the barn and slams him against the wall repeatedly. Mike is able to reach down and he still has the revolver from earlier, still with two bullets. He pulls the revolver from his pocket and squeezes the trigger, firing into Virgil's stomach, and then in his right thigh.

Virgil releases him immediately and falls onto the ground in pain. "Ahhh! I'm hit! He shot me! Jasper! Kill this motherf–! He shot me!" he cries as he holds onto the gunshot wound on his stomach. Mike staggers away from the wall and points the empty gun with weak aim at Jasper. Jasper comes at Mike and slaps the guns away and punches him in the face. Mike trips after the punch and falls backwards. He drops the gun and Jasper kicks it away.

Jasper stalks Mike who is crawling backwards, away from him. "You know, I gotta hand it to you kid… You got big fuckin' balls. I can't say I remember anyone puttin' up the fight that you have. It's a shame really that it has to end this way, like this. All this fighting, just to die like a dog anyway. Pathetic!" Jasper stands over Mike, who is slow to move, and he tilts his head to the left and then to the right to crack his neck and stretch. "Time to die!"

As Jasper closes in on Mike, the doors to the shed explode open and Jasper's attention turns to the abrupt sound of cracking and splintering wood slamming together. Olivia steps out wielding a gas-powered weed-eater. "Your watch is wrong, motherfucker!" She pulls the cord and the motor hums. Another pull of the cord and it fires right up. It is loud and definitely an equalizer.

Jasper backs up as Olivia walks toward him with the tool revved up, shouting as she holds down on the trigger. The weedeater has the edging blade attachment on so it's not plastic string spinning, it's a three sided metal piece that spins at ten thousand RPM and is designed to cut through soil, thicker weeds, shrubs and branches.

"Holy hell, you bitch! Put that thing down before you hurt yourself," Jasper advises as he backs away. Olivia continues to walk toward him and swings it at him. She waves it to her right as the blade spins. Olivia takes another swing and Jasper jumps back. Olivia is starting to laugh nervously. She is in control now and willing to do whatever it takes to survive, especially after seeing Nate in that shed just tossed into a wheelbarrow and hidden away for whatever they had planned for his body.

"Don't tell me you're scared now! I WOULDN'T WANT YOU TO BE SCARED!" Olivia screams as she runs at him. Jasper turns to run away and he trips over Virgil and falls on the ground.

"OW! AH! MY STOMACH!" Virgil screams as Jasper kicks and trips over him. Olivia ignores Virgil entirely as she hits Jasper in the foot and runs the humming power tool up his legs and into his lower back. He tosses around in agonizing pain. The spinning blade skips off of his flesh and jams up and she rips it away and starts it up again. Jasper lies on his side, crawling away by dragging himself with his forearm on the ground to pull his body across the ground.

"Ozzy! Patty! Help me!" he hollers into the night. "Okay! Okay! You win! I'm done! Just please, stop!" he pleads, as he holds out his hand to signal her to stop. His desperate pleading falls on deaf ears as Olivia swings the weed-eater with a lioness roar and takes off three of his fingers and part of his index finger.

He screams as he sees his hand become a fountain of his own blood. His fingers fly in different directions like blades of grass in a lawnmower. Jasper cries as he stares at the bloody mess of his hand in horror. His crying muddies up his voice as he starts to pray aloud. What he is saying is not really audible as Olivia stands over him. He looks away and covers his face.

"God isn't coming tonight. And God sure as hell isn't going to save you, YOU SICK FUCK!" Olivia screams as she shoves the weed-eater into his arm he uses to cover his face. With blood flinging from the spinning blade, he yanks his arm away as she shoves the weed-eater into the side of his head sending his ear flying off.

The side of his face that was burned not too long ago, is now the better-looking side of his face as she goes to work with the weed-eater, tearing through his cheek and his neck. It's not long before he stops resisting and his lifeless body is no longer in this fight. She screams in a flurry of rage, pressing the weed-eater into his face.

Mike gets to his feet and is in a lot of pain. He holds onto his ribs and picks up the empty revolver as he sees Olivia standing over Jasper's mutilated body. Olivia holds the power tool, exhausted. She is standing there trying to catch her breath as she is showered in blood. She looks over at Mike with her upper body moving like a ventilator with every deep breath. "Where's Ozzy? Where did he go?" Olivia asks.

"I-I don't know… Come on, we need to go," Mike urges Olivia, grimacing in pain.

Virgil is still sitting with his back against the barn as he holds onto his stomach. He leans over and is trying to scoot away slowly and sneakily. Olivia sees Virgil moving away and she becomes enraged again. She turns to him and pulls the trigger on the tool and jams the weed-eater into Virgil's chest. He goes limp pretty quickly and Olivia drops the power tool. Olivia hunches over with her hands on her knees, crying. "Liv, we've gotta go," Mike tells her with a hand on her shoulder.

As Olivia hangs her head, Mike is hit from behind with the stock of a rifle. Patty stands there holding the rifle with a scowl on her face. Mike stumbles forward and falls to one knee. Olivia turns to look and sees Patty holding the rifle. Before Patty can take aim, Olivia tackles her and slams her against the ground. The rifle is jarred loose and bounces off of the dirt. Olivia grabs Patty's hair on both sides of her head and she raises her head up and slams her head down onto the dirt. Patty kicks her legs to scoot away from Olivia enough to get some leverage to be able to toss Olivia onto her back. Patty is on top of Olivia, showing her clenching teeth as Patty's disheveled, blood-covered, ashy face stares down at her.

"You were supposed to bring God to us. You ruined that. YOU TOOK THAT FROM ME!" Patty yells with an intense tone. Patty has her hands around Olivia's neck, strangling her. Mike gets back to his feet and turns to Patty. He walks over to her and she sees his shadow and she turns around. Patty immediately lets go of Olivia and she reaches for the rifle. Mike sprints over to her, despite the pain he is in and as she bends to pick it up, he punt kicks her in the face and Patty collapses to the ground.

Olivia gets up and sees Patty start to get up. Olivia goes over to the shelving units that are along the back of the barn and she pulls one of these shelves down onto Patty. The shelving units tumble onto Patty and all of the things on each shelf come with it. Bones and animal pelts scatter across the ground. The collapsing shelves make a lot of noise.

Mike grabs Olivia's arm and pulls her away. "Come on. Let's get out of here!"

Olivia runs along Mike's side as the two limp away in a hurry, favoring various injuries and running on pure adrenaline. "We look for a car, if we can. We need to get out fast!' Mike says between his painful breathing. They hobble along the side of the barn with their eyes on the road. "We just have to get away from here." They make it to the open area that is in front of the barn. They both look around on high alert and they do not see anyone. They get about thirty feet away from the barn when one of the barn doors swings open. Ozzy steps out with a pitchfork in his hand. He sees Mike and Olivia moving away and he walks to the side of the barn to look for Patty.

Ozzy sees Jasper and Virgil lying in the dark, motionless. Patty emerges from the back of the shed, bloody, injured, off-balance, and shambling forward like a zombie as she carries a rifle. He turns and marches over to Mike and Olivia. "You can't run! Naw, naw, oh no. This is the devil's playground," he shouts. He stands with the barn at his back and Patty walking to join him at his side.

Olivia turns back and sees Patty with the rifle as she and Ozzy begin to walk toward them. "You've got to be kidding me! This bitch just won't die!" Olivia says, as she picks up the pace. Mike and Olivia are jogging as fast as they can with their tolerance for pain and physical discomfort being the only thing keeping them from being out of sight already.

"Just get to the road. We've made it this far. Just get to the road," Mike says as they drag themselves away.

30

◇

"That's right… Keep it movin', you'll get tired soon enough… And we'll be right there to scoop you up." Ozzy says, projecting loud enough for Mike and Olivia to hear him. They move as quickly as they can, with their backs to Ozzy and Patty.

"We've gotta get out of their view," Mike says to Olivia as he limps, holding his ribs.

"Just keep moving. If they want us, they're gonna have to work for it!" Olivia responds.

Ozzy walks very nonchalantly as Patty walks beside him, exhausted and in rough shape. "You doin' alright there my love? If you need to go get fixed up, I got this," Ozzy says, looking Patty up and down.

"I'm fine. Let's just catch these heathens so I can shower already," Patty responds as she walks with a look of determination on her face. "Let's take a car. Might be fun to run 'em down, we always talked about that," she says with a straight face as she looks ahead, not taking her eyes off of them.

Ozzy looks over at Patty with a smirk on his face. "Damn woman, well I'm not gonna tell you no. Choose your chariot my dear." Ozzy motions his arm toward a selection of battered, but mostly operational vehicles, like he is presenting a grand prize on a TV game show.

"Just get something that moves Oz. I'm tired," Patty says with an attitude.

Ozzy walks over to the vehicles and he looks at a white BMW that is filthy and looks like it's sat for a long time. "No…" Next to it is an early 2000's Malibu with a big crack in the windshield. "Nope…" A couple of cars down, there is a bright yellow, newer model Honda Civic. "Alright, now we're talking… Patty!" Ozzy hollers at Patty and waves her over. He crouches down behind the trunk of the car and feels around underneath. "There you are," he says as he finds the key and pulls off a magnetic key box and pulls the key out. He unlocks the doors with the keyfob and smiles as he hears the automatic locks disengage.

As Patty walks over, he goes to the passenger side of the car and opens the door. "M'lady…" he says sarcastically. Patty steps into the small car and Ozzy shuts the door. He tosses the pitchfork into the backseat, gets in, and starts it up.

Mike hears the car start as he and Olivia have reached the road and are not far from the gas station as they walk in the grass, along the shoulder of the road. Mike stops and tries to listen.

"Come on!" Olivia urges, frustrated as she continues.

"They've got a car. They're coming," Mike says with panic in his voice.

Olivia grabs Mike by his arm and pulls him, as she is eager to move. "COME ON! We can't stop!"

Ozzy is in the driver seat and puts the car in drive. "Hang on to your britches, honey!" he says to Patty as he drives out and turns to make their way to the road. With dirt kicking up clouds and the tires spinning out as he tears recklessly through the lot, Mike and Olivia continue running as fast as they can. With their injuries and them both limping, it is less like running and more like dragging each other.

"Yea-ha-hah! Woo!" Ozzy sings with childish enthusiasm as he whips the small car into the road. He turns on the headlights, creeping along the road in neutral, smashing the gas pedal to make the engine scream. The motor growls like a hungry animal ready to devour its next meal. Ozzy watches them ahead. Mike and Olivia see their shadows in front of them dancing on the ground as the lights behind them shine. The two turn back to see the blinding LED lights shining on them like they are the featuring act at a theater event. Ozzy and Patty have a front row seat and they only want to heckle the stars as Ozzy flashes the brights with the car idling in neutral.

Mike picks up his pace a little more, grimacing in discomfort with each step he takes. Olivia stays close to him but is in better shape and able to move around a little better. They hear the engine revving and see the flashing brights, but keep their eyes ahead.

"Should we try to duck off into the grass?" Mike asks, nodding to his right at the field of crops. They consider going into the field but there is chicken wire fencing up, keeping them from easily ducking out of sight. Olivia turns back and the headlights flashing almost feel like laughter. Ozzy mashes the pedal and the tires sing against the pavement as the small car takes off in a hurry.

"They're coming!" Olivia screams as she jerks Mike's arm. The car takes no time at all speeding down the road. Ozzy grips the steering wheel tightly with intent and focus in his eyes. He keeps Mike and Olivia in his line of sight and the headlights behind them. He puts his hand on the emergency brake and licks his lips as he tries to run them down. Mike and Olivia see he is not stopping or slowing down and they both jump out of the way, barely. As Ozzy passes them he aggressively pulls the steering wheel as hard to the left as he can and hits the emergency brake, causing the car to do a one eighty spin and he comes to a complete stop with the car in the middle of the road. The headlights are on Mike and Olivia as they crawl and get to their feet.

Ozzy puts the car in park with the engine running as he and Patty open the doors and step out. Ozzy turns around and reaches into the backseat for his pitchfork and he spins it a few times as he steps out in front of the car and stares deviously at Mike and Olivia. Patty is by his side with the rifle. Mike and Olivia stand there with nowhere to really run to now. They both hold their forearms over their eyes to see Ozzy and Patty's silhouettes in the bright lights. Ozzy takes a few steps forward and as he takes steps, he uses the pitchfork like it is a walking stick as the handle clacks against the concrete.

"You know… I think I speak for the both of us when I say, we're kind of tired of chasing you two. This might be a good time to just be done with you both and… Well… try again next time," Ozzy says with a little bit of disappointment in his tone. Mike and Olivia stand silently with a sense of uneasiness and just total exhaustion from the night.

Patty begins to take steps away from Ozzy and she points the rifle at Olivia. "You know, I wasn't going to kill you because

I enjoy it," Patty says with aggravation drawn all over her bloodied face. Patty loads the rifle as she is talking to Olivia. "But now… Just know, I'm going to enjoy this. I really, really am."

Ozzy holds up a hand. "Stop!" he says. Patty points the rifle to the ground and rolls her eyes. Ozzy takes a few steps toward Mike and Olivia as they stand there anticipating his next move. They have nowhere to go, no weapons, and no plan. Ozzy stands about six feet away from Olivia, holding the pitchfork, looking her up and down. "You know, we were so close," Ozzy says, holding up his hand with his index finger and thumb almost touching with hatred in his eyes. "I had a feeling, oh boy did I have a feeling that you might be the one," he says to Olivia as he begins to slowly pace in the road "Ugh! I should have just killed you as soon as we let you run. I mean, I killed your shithead boyfriend right in front of y'all. Of course, of freakin' *course* you were going to be angry… That's my bad. Stupid me!" he says with animated body language. His arms, matching the charisma and emotion of his spiel. "Now, you've gone and killed a handful of my friends. You've really messed up my wife's beautiful face, and for what? All we wanted to do was invite God into our lives."

Ozzy's facial expressions, ever-changing, are unpredictable. A man of performance, you might think, as he seems to adore any audience who will hear him talk. You can sense sarcasm and pain in his voice all at once.

"This ceremony was going to be perfect, oh it was going to be magnificent! It was so simple really. Capture the entitled youth, check. Surround yourself with a community of loved ones who have let God into their hearts, check. Bless and clean the flesh and consume the wicked as God walks in and loves us unconditionally…" Ozzy pauses and looks directly at Mike. "You kept us from God." He turns to Olivia. "Now you have to die… I mean, you were always going to die, but it's just now, it's a wasted death… And now I'm… I'm just pissed off."

Patty looks over at Ozzy, very impatiently. "Jesus Christ Ozzy, would you just cut the shit. I need to get my face looked at."

"Alright, alright, sorry… You know how I get sometimes, honey," Ozzy says with a smirk on his face. "Well I guess this is it then… You two die just like the rest of 'em."

"You seem to talk a lot about God, but you are not a man of God," Olivia says with a look of despair and disgust.

Ozzy laughs, "That's valid, I guess. Maybe I'm just the devil trying to get back." Ozzy looks over to Patty and nods his head toward her. "And she is my fire… And you two played with fire tonight. I think now it's only right that-" As Ozzy is talking, Mike summons up a burst of energy and lunges forward, tackling Ozzy.

31

◇

Ozzy is taken to the ground by Mike. Olivia and Patty are caught completely off guard by Mike's last ditch effort to survive. Olivia looks over to see Patty taking aim at Mike, and she tackles her. As Ozzy slams against the unforgiving concrete, Mike is quick to climb on top of him and goes for his throat. With one hand gripping his throat and the other hand fighting to do the same, Ozzy reaches up to fight back, squeezing Mike's wrist as he resists. Mike squeezes Ozzy's throat while trying to pull his other hand free and he leans in close to Ozzy's face, applying as much of his own weight and pressure to his strangling.

Olivia wrestles with Patty on the hard, worn and weathered road. Olivia lets out loud screams and yelps with every burst of adrenaline. The rifle is knocked loose and just out of reach. Patty digs her fingernails into Olivia's leg where the piece of skin was taken off. Olivia shrieks in agony. Olivia is thrown off and lies on the ground in pain. As Mike stares into the eye of the man who murdered his best friends earlier tonight, he focuses all of his anger and hurt into making sure Ozzy suffers. Mike's rage transcends seeking justice. He wants Ozzy to understand that he is making a choice to kill him now. The events of this evening have changed him. The trauma will go on with him after tonight. There is no going back and he wants Ozzy to know what mark he has left on him.

Ozzy struggles and as he gasps for air he thrusts his hips up and digs his feet into the ground, bucking like a bull to try and throw Mike off. As Mike tries to stay on, Ozzy allows enough movement to be able to reach his head up and bite Mike's hand. Mike pulls his hand away as quickly as he can while Ozzy coughs and chokes, trying to breathe again. Mike tries to ignore the bite and the blood that is leaking from his hand now as he reaches down and grabs the side of Ozzy's face and turns his head away, pinning him down. Mike yells throughout the struggle and that is when he is struck in the back of the head. *CRACK!* Mike falls over onto the road, releasing Ozzy, who scampers away, and gets to his feet quickly as he massages his neck and hacks up a lung after being strangled. Patty stands over Mike with the rifle she just hit him with and now she is pointing it at him. "Don't move boy," she says to him.

Olivia lies on her side in pain trying to muster the strength to do something heroic. Dawn is breaking as the sun peeks through the grass and crops around them. Olivia watches Patty aim a rifle while standing over Mike, who lies on the ground, in a fetal position, holding onto the back of his head. She sees Ozzy on his feet with his back to everyone, hunched over spitting and trying to clear his throat, as he is cursing between coughing fits. She stares at Patty's feet and then stares at the ground. She focuses on the cracks in the road and the spots where the road can be a bit bumpy from the missing pieces of surface pavement. She fixates on a patch of tattered and beaten road where there are loose chunks of concrete, clumps of the road that just sit like the wrong pieces to a puzzle, bouncing around as cars drive over them, day after day.

Olivia reaches out, pulling herself onto her stomach, and she grabs a chunk of the road. Maybe six or seven inches long, and shaped like the state of New Jersey. She pulls herself to her feet, as fast as she can, with a piece of the road in her hand. She walks over intently and raises her hand above her head, and swings the chunk of cement down with precision into the top of Patty's skull. Patty crouches down, surprised as she fumbles the rifle and tries to get a grip on it and before she could turn around to see what just hit her, Olivia lets out a warrior cry, swinging the concrete with a left hook and hitting an already dazed Patty in the side of the head. Patty collapses to the ground, motionless and bleeding.

Ozzy turns around to see Olivia standing there, with desperation in her eyes and survival being her only goal now. He sees Patty lying on the ground, not moving, and looks back to Olivia who is holding a big rock in her hand.

"Patty… Baby… Get up now," Ozzy says, shaken up. Patty is nonresponsive and blood is pooling underneath her head as she lies there. Olivia looks at Ozzy as she breathes heavily. Mike is trying to get to his feet. He gets to his knees and the pain he is in can be seen across his face as he struggles to move. He gets to his feet and he turns to see Olivia standing over Patty.

Ozzy quickly walks over and picks up the pitchfork and walks over to Mike. "Fuck this. You're all fucking dead!" Ozzy proclaims as he pulls the pitchfork back and with a swift motion pushes all four rusted prongs of the pitchfork into Mike's back.

"Noooo!" Olivia screams in terror as she sees Mike's facial expression jolt into a wide-eyed, pain-induced moment of paralysis.

Mike stares down and sees the pointy ends of the prongs protruding from his chest and abdomen. He coughs and blood spurts out of his mouth a little as he looks at Olivia. "I- I'm sorry… Run, p-please!" Olivia stands crying, watching as Ozzy yanks the pitchfork clean out of Mike's back with his eyes on her now.

Ozzy's gaze pierces through Olivia as the dawn's sun whispers onto his back. He looks like a monster gripping the pitchfork with both hands as blood runs down the prongs. Ozzy shakes his head no as he begins to walk toward Olivia. "You stupid fucking whore, LOOK WHAT YOU'VE DONE!" Mike falls forward onto his knees and as Ozzy is walking by him, Mike grabs onto his pant leg. Ozzy jerks his leg away quickly and he stops and turns around to Mike and Mike raises up from his knees and Ozzy, without hesitation reaches back and sinks the business end of the pitchfork into the center mass of Mike's chest. Mike gasps from the sudden penetration. He looks Ozzy in the eyes and he coughs up more blood. Ozzy stares down at him. "Let's see how God treats you now motherfucker!" He puts his foot against Mike's chest and pushes against his body with his foot as he pulls the pitchfork out of his chest.

Mike falls over immediately and rolls onto his back, choking on his blood as he looks to the sky, focusing on the pink fading into the dark blue from the sun rising. Mike has accepted his fate as he watches his last sunrise. Ozzy steps over him and now is the only thing he sees. "Lights out forever!" he says just before he raises the pitchfork up and plunges it down into Mike's face. Two of the points go into his right cheek near his left eye. Ozzy spits on Mike's face and pulls the pitchfork out, turning to Olivia.

Olivia sobs as she throws the rock at Ozzy and makes a run toward the car that is still running with the doors open. Ozzy tenses up and takes the hit in the shoulder, unphased. He gives chase and she manages to get into the driver's seat just in time and shut the door. Ozzy smacks onto the window and stares her down. "Get out of the damn car you little bitch!" He smacks the window again, even harder. The rings on his hand make a loud impact on the window and Olivia flinches as he hits it. Each time he smacks the glass she is sure it breaks but it doesn't. "Get the fuck out here right now! You killed my wife! Now I'm gonna kill you!" Ozzy goes to the other side and Olivia leans over and pulls that door shut. Ozzy tries to open the door and continues his tantrum.

He swings the pitchfork like it's a baseball bat onto the hood of the car. Olivia flinches and screams. "GET THE FUCK OUT!" Ozzy howls. He goes over to the driver side and takes another big, homerun swing, this time at the window. Olivia puts the car in drive and mashes the pedal just as the pitchfork connects with the window, breaking it into tiny shards of glass that fall into her lap, onto her seat, behind her back, and onto the floor of the car. He runs alongside the car while it is accelerating, he thrusts the pitchfork into the rear driver's side tire, popping it. Olivia watches in the mirrors but keeps driving. Ozzy stands in the middle of the road, watching her drive away as she watches him in the mirror.

The tire shreds and tatters with pieces flying off as she reaches faster speeds. It's not long before she is riding on a bare rim and scraping it against the pavement, creating sparks and loud grinding noises. "No, no, no, no, NO!" Olivia cries as she struggles to control the steering. She slows the car down and the car fishtails before veering off into the grass on the shoulder of the road. She gets about the length of a football field away before she stops the car from crashing and without hesitation she turns the engine off, removes the key, and gets out and starts to run. Panic clashes with adrenaline and Olivia's only goal now is escape. She looks over her shoulder, after she tosses the car key into the tall sunflowers that are across the street, and sees Ozzy walking toward her, but he is a safe distance from her. Given the way that the night has unfolded up to this point, she isn't taking any chances. She may never feel safe again after this.

32

◇

Ozzy stands in the road, watching Olivia drive away while he follows in that direction for a moment before realizing it's a waste of time to bother chasing. "God dammit!" he shouts, in a fit of rage before he launches his pitchfork deep into a field like it were a spear. He runs his hands through his hair, visibly agitated and at his wit's end, looking around at the scene.

Ozzy looks over and sees Mike's body and the mess he has made. He then looks over to his wife, who lies there in a slow pooling puddle of blood from the impact to her head. Ozzy goes to Patty and sits down beside her and rests her head in his hands delicately as he stares at her beaten and bruised mess of a face. He begins to weep. "I love you. I'm going to make this right. I promise." Tears stream down his face and he quickly becomes angry again. "You don't get to just die! Please, don't leave me alone."

Ozzy wipes her face and stares at her, sad and angry. He leans down and kisses her lips before he carries her over to the side of the road and sets her gingerly in the grass. He realizes that it looks exactly like what it is right now, and the sun is coming up quickly. It looks very blatantly like a murder scene in the daylight. He walks over and grabs the rifle and tosses it into the tall grass, and then he drags Mike's body off of the road.

He stares at the mess of blood on the road and sighs. He reaches to the walkie talkie on his waist. "Homebase, do you have a copy? Over." He waits for a moment for a reply.

The voice of a woman comes over the radio. "Go for Homebase."

"I need a few hands to come out here for some cleanup. Water, deck brush, bleach, a couple wheel burrows, the whole nine. Over," Ozzy says.

"Yessir. On the way. Over."

Ozzy gets back on the walkie. "Listen up. Tell everyone, right now, we need them to come out right now. I need a car. We need to find the girl. Our preservation depends on it. She is getting away. We've lost too much to just let her get away now. EVERYONE. OUT. NOW!" Ozzy announces, firmly. Ozzy stands around for a moment, hoping that no motorists drive by while he waits for his people. It's not long at all before a pickup truck comes and stops for him to climb in.

The older man driving looks at Ozzy. He notices the bruising on his neck and the blood all over him. "Shit, son, what the hell happened out here?"

Ozzy stares at the road ahead. "Just drive."

The man sighs, putting the truck in gear as they drive, sitting in silence as Ozzy looks around on high alert. They approach the Honda Civic that Olivia took. Ozzy sees the car with the driver side door open. "Pull over." Ozzy hops out and checks inside the car. He notices the keys are gone. He looks around and doesn't see Olivia anywhere.

Another car pulls up alongside the truck and a man in the passenger seat rolls the window down. "What are we lookin' for Oz?"

Ozzy is walking back to the truck. "The girl. She's hurt so she can't be moving too quickly. No cars have come through either so she's gotta be close."

"Alright boss," the man says as he bangs on the top of the car. 'Let's go!" The car drives ahead, on the search for Olivia.

Olivia runs, while limping up the road and hears the cars behind her driving her way. She ducks off, down a gravel driveway of a farm. She drags her injured leg across the gravel and runs into a field. She moves through the crops and tall stalks in a hurry, but makes a lot of noise in the process. Birds take off as she comes close to flocks of them in the field.

The car ahead of Ozzy pulls over and he sees the birds taking off in the field. He focuses on the crops and sees a lot of movement. "Bingo! …Pull over. I think we got her," Ozzy says with a newfound confidence. Ozzy hops out of the vehicle and draws the gun from the back of his waistband and is brandishing it openly now. The two men from the other vehicle run into the field in the direction that the birds are flying from. Ozzy and his driver are right behind them. "Be alert. This bitch knows we're after her and she will do anything to get away," Ozzy says to his driver.

Olivia moves through the field, breathing heavily, covered in blood and grime. She is aware of the noise she is making and notices the birds flying out as she moves through. She sees the end of the crops up ahead and sees a clearing. She reaches the edge of the crops and carefully steps out. She looks around to see fields of weeds and grass that do not seem to be manicured as often. About a hundred yards away, just across the natural brush and weeds there are tall trees. She makes her way to the trees in hopes of finding cover, or a brief refuge or, at the very least, to catch her breath. She leans against a tree and looks out behind her and sees movement in the fields she was just in. She is panicked all over again knowing just how close they are to her.

Olivia's pursuers come out of the field and into the clearing and are looking around.

"Do we go into the woods?" one of the men asks.

"She ain't going anywhere else. If she ain't there, we'd see her," Ozzy replies.

The men march ahead, across the field of wild weeds and messy patches of grass, into the woods. The dawning sunshine peers over the horizon and illuminates the trees and shines through the leaves. Olivia is in the woods running. Surrounded by trees, fallen and standing, birds singing their morning song as squirrels run along trees, the setting has become an oxymoron for the terror that is nipping at her heels. She weaves through branches and tree limbs stepping over fallen trees. She is able to see through the trees just ahead that she is close to another clearing. She stumbles and pushes through until she comes out of the other side.

Ozzy and his men move quickly through the woods when one of the men stops.

"What is it?" Ozzy asks.

The man puts his index and middle finger to his eyes and then points in the direction ahead where they see Olivia moving through. Ozzy pats the man on the shoulder a few times and then holds his fist out for a fist bump. The man smiles and bumps it as Ozzy motions his hand forward. With the gun in hand and eyes on Olivia, Ozzy and his gang are dead-set on killing her and being done with this failed ritual.

Olivia comes out and she sees train tracks just ahead. Her eyes light up with a sense of hope that she has not had at any point throughout the last eight hours or so. She darts off as fast as she can across the field that is a short distance between her and the tracks but as she gets closer she realizes that there is a fence separating her from the tracks. Her reinvigorated hope turns back to desperation as she reaches the fence. She looks in both directions and is unsure which way to go. While she is deciding, she hears a rustling and movement in the trees behind her. She turns back to see several men and Ozzy coming out, and they have their sights set on her. "Shit!" she says to herself as she decides very quickly to go right. She runs along the fence as the men give chase. Ozzy fires a shot and the sound rings out with an echo. Anyone who might have heard it is either back at the barn, looking for Olivia or assumed it was a hunter out hunting deer.

The shot misses her but she knows that he means business and she wants no part of that. As she hobbles along, practically dragging her injured leg, the much welcomed sound of a train horn blows in the distance from behind her. This is music to her ears as she knows that she just has to find a way to get near the tracks, but to do that, she also has to outpace those men that are after her. She looks back and sees a man sprinting toward her and he is much quicker than her. "No… Shit!… Please, please, please, no!" she says as she keeps moving. She sees up ahead where it looks like the fence had been repaired with wire. She stops and tries to tear it off but it is tight. She looks around and sees a rock and she reaches down for it. She uses the rock like a knife and with a couple of hard swings, the wire is severed and the fence comes apart, revealing the door to her salvation. She squeezes through the opening in the fence and runs along the tracks.

The man is not far behind her and she knows that she will have to resort to a fight if he catches her, and judging by his speed, she will have to fight. She looks around the tracks and as she is running sees mostly gravel. She is running and sees an old railroad spike lying on the outside of the tracks on the wood. Without much thought, she instinctively picks it up as the man run's up behind her. As fast as he gets to her, she springs up, turning to stick the railroad spike right in his eye. The man falls down to one knee, screaming. His hands shaking, unsure what he is to do. "Get it out, get it out!" the man cries. He very tenderly grabs the head of the spike and Olivia doesn't stick around to watch.

Ozzy and the other men catch up to the man with the spike. "Whoa there. Let me look at that before you go taking it–" Ozzy says to the man just as he pulls it out of his eye. One of the men pukes at the sight of his eyes and the mixture of blood and what looks like mucus.

"God DAMMIT!" Ozzy screams. He walks away from his injured brother and takes aim at Olivia who is a couple hundred yards away. He takes another shot at her and misses again. "Fuck!" he says. He turns back to the men tending to their brother, who sits on the rail crying. "I'm gonna go after her. You guys can take him back." As Ozzy focuses his full attention on Olivia he begins to jog. As he is jogging the train horn blows again. This time it is a lot closer. "You stupid little- Your ass is mine," Ozzy says under his breath. He picks up his pace a bit as he turns back and can now see the train behind them in the distance. The train horn blows again.

Olivia is giving her all until this train comes. She moves onto the tracks and looks back to see Ozzy chasing her, and he is gaining speed. He aims the gun and she looks forward and flinches as a shot rings out. The bullet ricochets off of the rail to her right and creates sparks. She shrieks as an involuntary reaction to the gunshot, turning back again seeing that Ozzy is getting winded and slowing down, but he isn't stopping. She also sees the train approaching as it's horn blows once more. She steps to her left to be on the other side of the tracks. Ozzy does the same. The train horn blows once more and is rolling quickly. It is not far behind her now and she knows that the only way she can feasibly make it out alive is if she can manage to catch this train somehow, someway.

Exhaustion is beginning to sink in and her legs are in absolute pain. Muscles are weakening and fatigue is setting in. Her chest is cold from breathing in deep breaths for so long, her body is not conditioned for the marathon she has run. She realizes that this is it and that she just has to make it a little longer as things are in slow motion for her at this point. The intensity of the moment paints the scene, a defining moment of her very survival. She knows in her heart that she has to do everything she can to survive to tell her story and to seek justice against this sick cult of rednecks. She must live on for her friends. Their families can't go on wondering why they will never see them again. *This is it.*

The train horn blows once more. It has arrived. Olivia uses a final burst of energy and trickery, and, at the last possible moment, as the train has passed Ozzy already, she hops the tracks and shuffles across with the train just barely missing as the horn blows once more. She falls to the ground as she jumps out of the way of the train just in time. Ozzy is on the other side and he is looking under the train and sees Olivia. He aims the gun but is unable to get a clear shot because of the wheels rolling and the angle he is at. Olivia sees him watching her and she smiles as the relief sets in, accompanied by involuntary laughter. She gives him the middle finger and climbs back to her feet.

The train is moving quickly and there are a lot of train cars in motion. She waits for an opportunity to be able to grab onto a ladder that hangs on the side but the train is moving too fast. Several train cars with ladders zip by her. She mentally prepares herself to grab onto one and knows that once she grabs on she has to hold on for dear life and use every ounce of strength to pull herself onto the ladder and hold on tight. She closes her eyes and tries to calm her nerves before reaching out. She opens her eyes and the train seems to be moving even faster now. She sees a ladder coming up and she readies herself letting out a yell as she reaches out to grab on. She launches herself off the ground and is whisked away in a hurry.

She hangs on like she has never hung on to anything before. The wheels barreling over the tracks and hundreds of tons of steel moving through like a stampede. She gets both hands onto the rungs of the ladder and is able to stabilize her feet. She clings close to the train, scared, shaking, and surprised at herself. She lets out a laugh. Not a happy laugh, but an 'I can't believe I actually pulled this off' kind of laugh. Olivia looks back and doesn't see anyone as she rides away to safety. She rides her industrial chariot out of hell and is more than happy to go anywhere this train takes her. Her hanging on the side of this moving train is the most calm she has had in a while.

She thinks about what she will say when the train stops and someone sees her. *What do I tell the police? What do I tell my family? My friend's parents?* She needs a hospital. So many things run through her head while she rides away. Whatever happens though, she knows what happened here and she knows she will have to carry this with her for the rest of her life.

33

◇

Olivia sits on a dark green vinyl loveseat in a doctor's office as she picks at the cuticles on her thumbs nervously. The young female doctor sits in an office chair with her legs crossed, a legal pad on her lap, and an ink pen resting against her cheek as she listens to Olivia.

"And are you still having nightmares?" the therapist calmly asks.

Olivia looks away from her fidgeting hands and stares out the window. "Yeah, It's the same every time. Always the same. I can't sleep. I haven't had a full night of sleep in months. I'm a mess, I know."

The therapist takes a short note on her legal pad. "Tell me again, about the nightmares."

Olivia sighs as she leans back with brief hesitation. "I'm with Nate. We're holding hands, just walking, Kris and Mike are there, we're at a celebration, like, Independence Day or something. There's fireworks, everyone is… Everyone is happy." Olivia begins to feel her eyes well up. She wipes her eyes with the back of her hand and the therapist passes her the box of tissues.

"Thank you," Olivia says as she takes the box. She pulls a few sheets of tissue and sets the box beside her on the loveseat as she continues with her story. "Everyone is happy, everyone is having a good time, there's music… I look away from the fireworks for a second and I'm standing there. Nate is beside me singing along to a song and I can see Mike and Kris enjoying themselves. I look forward, into the crowd. And I see him."

"Who do you see?" the therapist asks.

Olivia looks at the therapist with certainty in her eyes. "The devil."

The therapist is writing in her legal pad. "Tell me more about the devil you see."

Olivia rubs her knees as she sits there. "He's not like the devil with the horns and the tail. None of that stuff you read in books or hear about in movies. I see Ozzy. From that night."

"And what is Ozzy doing, in your dream?" the therapist asks.

With a deep breath, Olivia focuses back on looking out the window as she recalls the dreams. 'He is just staring at me… Everyone in the crowd is looking up and forward and he is just standing there. With his back to the fireworks… Staring at me. No! He's staring *through* me… Like he is peering into my soul."

The therapist taps on her leg with the pen as she listens. "What does it feel like when he looks at you?"

Olivia wipes her eyes with tissue. "It's like… I can feel my chest tightening. My throat closes up. And before I know it I'm just standing there, all alone." Olivia begins to cry a bit more as she is describing this nightmare she routinely has. "And he just stares a hole right through me. And I- I try to speak and I can't.

Words don't come out. I try to move and it's like the ground moves away from me. He starts walking toward me and the sky falls and just before he gets to me I wake up. Sweaty. My parents, at times, standing there at the foot of my bed. They tell me I scream in my sleep sometimes… I don't know what to tell them. I'm sorry. I'm sorry that I keep having these fucking nightmares. I never asked for this."

"Let's touch base on some other areas in your life," the therapist suggests, sensing the heaviness in the room. Talk to me about school and work."

"Work?" Olivia chuckles. "How can I work?"

The therapist writes on her notepad. "What about school? You mentioned to me a few weeks back that you were working on finishing school."

"Well, I am actually enrolled for the next semester, so we will see," Olivia replies with uncertainty in her voice.

"That's great to hear! Are you nervous?" the therapist asks.

Olivia shrugs. "A little bit, yeah."

"Well… I think it is important that you continue to try and get back to normal things. Get back to living your life. And while you work on those things, we will address some of the things you mentioned to me. The guilt, the anger, and the anxiety you have. You've been through a lot, but you have also grown a lot. I am proud of the work we've done over the months that you've been coming in to see me," the therapist says with a pleasant smile and eyes that are disarming.

"Thank you," Olivia says.

The therapist sets the legal pad on the table beside her before looking at her watch. "I think this is a good place to stop. Let's call it a day. Go on, get out of here. Go grab lunch."

Olivia stands up and begins to gather her things. "I'm actually heading to my parents in a bit."

"That sounds lovely," the doctor says.

"Yeah," Olivia replies.

The doctor looks at Olivia with a polite smirk. "Well I will see you next Wednesday."

"I'll be here."

"Alright Olivia, take care now."

"Bye," Olivia replies as she walks out of the office and makes her way to her car. This appointment was one of the two appointments Olivia attends every week now. She also sees a psychiatrist who prescribes her the medicine that helps her function close to normal. Olivia gets in her car and shuts the door as she starts the car and sits there for a moment with her eyes closed, listening to the song on the radio playing at a lower volume. She opens her eyes and stares at her legs. She looks at the spot on her leg where the skin was removed in the barn last summer. It has since healed up nicely after she received medical attention. She recently got her leg tattooed with three birds, carrying prayer beads that wrap tastefully around her thigh and hip. It is a very detailed piece that nearly hides the scar entirely. She figured she always had wanted a tattoo and this might be easier to look at than the scarring from that night. She looks at her cell phone and sees that she has a missed call and a voicemail. She taps on the voicemail notification and it plays over her car's bluetooth.

"Hey Liv, it's Mom. Your father and sister and I know you are coming home later today. We just wanted to see what you

were hungry for and we will make you whatever you would like. You've just been so busy lately and when you're home, you're holed up in your room. We're all so proud of you and are happy you're going back to school. I know you're living back home but we never see you hardly, it feels like… Oh sheesh, would you look at me, I'm rambling now. I'm sorry sweetie. We just miss you is all. But hey. Listen. We love you so much and can't wait to see you. Okay. Buh-bye."

She sits for a moment and grins subtly as she backs out of the parking spot and turns onto the road, well on her way home. She actively focuses on positive things and listens to upbeat music and the closer she gets to being home, the more she is beginning to look forward to it. She has been working hard to find inner peace and also recognizing when she needs to just change her scenery. She tries to avoid thinking about that night. She doesn't think about the arrests that followed the events. She tries not to think about the people who are still out there. She doesn't think about the cache of illegal weapons found or the dozens of human remains found on the property. The news reports and evening TV specials that spawned from the story of her surviving that night. She is just focused on smiling and bringing productive and positive energy into the rest of her day.

She pulls into the driveway and sees her mom's van, her dad's SUV, and her sister's Kia Soul. She gathers her things and gets out of the car and walks to the front door, actively trying to have a good, positive attitude. She opens the front door and announces herself, "Guuuys! …I'm hooome." She walks into the foyer and straight ahead is the kitchen. No one is in there. Through the kitchen, into the dining room, she walks in and drops her bag onto the floor. Her lip begins to quiver. Her voice cracks as she tries to speak but she is rendered speechless.

Olivia stands there in horror, as she looks at a set table for four, and her father lays on the carpet, bloody. There is evidence of a struggle. His face is bloody and bruised and his throat cut. Olivia's hands cover her mouth and she looks at her sister whose headless body lies underneath a chair, and the head is sitting upright in the seat that the body is under. On the wall on the other end of the table, her mom is fixed to the wall, crucified by a series of knives and large roofing nails. She has them in her hands, her shoulders, ankles, her thighs, and one right in the front of her neck. Her mom's eyes are still open with a blank stare, looking into the kitchen behind Olivia.

There is so much blood and Olivia is mortified. She falls to her knees and belts out a slow cry that makes no noise at first before she is overcome with emotion. She sits at her sister's feet and holds her. She screams and is confused as to what this is. *Is this even real? This can't be real... Can it?* She stands up and notices that on the table is a cell phone. She sees that it is her old phone... The one she had last summer... The one that was taken from her by Virgil on the road that night.

The screen is lit up and it shows a GPS map and the red dot of where they are. In the search bar on the GPS app it simply says 'Home.' Olivia's worst night ever has returned as she puts the pieces together. Underneath the phone there is a handwritten note.

The note reads...

"YOU TOOK PEOPLE FROM ME - SO I TOOK EVERYTHING FROM YOU. FAMILY IS EVERYTHING. WELCOME HOME. SEE YOU SOON."

Olivia backs away from the dining room in complete horror, in tears and disbelief of this revelation. All of her paranoia has become real and everything she has worked to overcome has been reborn. Her deafening cries carry out loud and would send a chill up anyone's spine. Olivia falls to the floor and sits in the corner, breaking down, staring at the bodies of more of her loved ones. Olivia survived that night… But at what cost?

THE END

Epilogue

◇

After Olivia rode off on the train, she hung on until it made a stop in Chattanooga, Tennessee. From there, she climbed down and arrived in a shipping yard where she was able to find help from one of the workers on site. She contacted the police and explained everything and then waited for her parents to pick her up from a police station in Chattanooga.

When she got home, it wasn't until the next day when she met with the families of Nathan, Kris, and Mike and tried to share what happened as sugar-coated as she could. Eventually they would read about the events online and in the local newspapers, and then hear about it on the news where it made national headlines. After she was home for just a few days, all of the parents held a candlelight vigil in the community, which was televised remembering those who died that night.

Police arrived after receiving a call from a concerned, passing motorist who was passing through on SR 49, when they reported an accident and multiple battered cars and fresh glass on the road and what looked like blood. Police arrived and an investigation began immediately. During these investigations, Patty and Mike's bodies were the first to be found in the weeds, close to the wreckage. Later in the morning they got word that Olivia had arrived in Chattanooga by way of train, escaping this crime scene. She became the prime witness and she filled in the gaps to most of the questions that law enforcement had on the scene.

Police showed up at the gas station that afternoon and the owner, Robert Mullins, was questioned and arrested on the spot for involvement in the events. Officers then raided and searched the compound behind the property and at least a dozen arrests were made. Upon questioning, most of them were pretty quiet about everything and demanded to speak to their lawyers but a few were willing to cooperate. Some of those arrested were in the middle of destroying evidence while others managed to flee. Many of them were physically unable to fight or run and just submitted to authorities.

Several of those questioned at the compound revealed the farmhouse nearby where Ben, Cassie, Kenny, and Twinkie's bodies were left. Tom was found in the fields as well, not far from his vehicle that had spun out off of the road.

Over seventy five guns were seized, along with illegal and unregistered weapons. Many of the vehicles found in the lot were missing their VIN but police were still able to compare vehicles reported missing or stolen with what they could, and also verify that some of those vehicle owners had been reported missing. Many of the vehicles reported missing had been missing for nearly ten years.

Several bodies were found on the property that were from that night. Also other remains were found, including bones and meat that was carefully packaged in a deep freezer.

In the upper level, there was a vanity desk that was being used as an altar in the corner that seemed to be dedicated to God, and on this altar there was a drawer that had over forty wallets, and additionally loose driver licenses and student IDs. This proved incredibly helpful in solving many open missing person reports over the last decade.

After the initial questioning of the suspects arrested, it was revealed that this cult was entirely made up of the senior community nearby, led by Oswald Peterson AKA Ozzy, military veteran and respected church leader. He still remains missing with several other members of the group who were reported to be involved as well.

Acknowledgements

I want to thank anyone who has ever listened to me think out loud while I rant about my ideas and things I want to try. There are a lot of you. Some of you are just being polite and I'm not so naive to think everyone is interested, but some of you are enablers and I appreciate that. That support goes a long way with stimulating these things.

I want to acknowledge my rock, my partner, and love of my life, Kaylynn, who has always been supportive of whatever venture I find myself obsessing over. You see and hear about these obsessions and see behind the curtain and I know you don't always understand what I'm talking about but you still let me dance on my soapbox and even feed into it at times and for that I love you. Thank you.

I want to thank those who were willing to be alpha/beta readers and help me shape this book into what it is. I realize how important it is to have a few people willing to read my work and pick it apart constructively and that willingness is invaluable. It is not lost on me that asking someone to read an entire novel; that isn't even published yet is a big ask. Thank you.

A big thanks to Barry and Shane for helping me with the concept photography, props, and location scouting. This was a huge help in making this book (the first edition) look how I wanted it to look. Thanks fellas.

Thank you to the people I've met through Instagram during this journey who helped me with different resources when needed or offered insight and suggestions.

I want to thank anyone who is reading this book also. Are you reading this right now? Well geez, this is uncomfortable now… Thanks and stuff…

Anyhow… Whether you bought it online, bought it from me personally, found it lying somewhere and thought to yourself '*Hmm, this seems interesting*', stole it from your sibling, was a gift, whatever… Thank you. Seriously. It takes a lot of work to write a book and self-publish it, and then you start down that path and realize you need a team, support, and in the end, you need readers.

About The Author

David Washburn is an aspiring author from Cincinnati, Ohio. With two boys at home. He has dipped his toe in writing short stories and screenplays and sporadically writes a guest blog for a baseball website. He has always been a creative person who has dabbled in many things, but never really went *all-in* on any one skill.

David is a big fan of horror films, but enjoys a little bit of everything. Fitness and staying active are a big part of his routine and he is always trying to stay creative, whether it be drawing, painting, writing, photography, or random home projects inspired by things he has seen on social media when the motivation strikes.

If you enjoyed this novel, please take a moment to review it on Amazon, Barnes & Noble, Goodreads, and anywhere else it is available. This helps indie authors a great deal with improving and learning what works for the readers. It also helps bring in more readers.